choose

this

now

choose this now

nicole haroutunian

Published by Noemi Press, Inc. A Nonprofit Literary Organization.
www.noemipress.org

Cover Image is © Caroline McAuliffe
Cover & Book Design by co•im•press

ISBN: 978-1-955992-03-9

for my friends

CONTENTS

1 · TWENTY-ONE

13 · POINTS OF LIGHT

34 · TWENTY-SIX

42 · DECISION MAKING FOR SAFE
AND HEALTHY LIVING

53 · CLEAR BLUE

68 · LANDMARK DECISIONS

83 · DAY JOBS

102 · SHALLOW LATCH

123 · LIFEGUARDS

142 · THIRTY-TWO

148 · SATURDAY, NEW YORK CITY

164 · PARCHED

177 · JESUS LOUISE

190 · SEAS BETWEEN US

211 · THIRTY-FIVE

221 · AFTER AMERICA

241 · ACKNOWLEDGMENTS

TWENTY-ONE
Valerie, 1999

THE PARTY IS OFF-CAMPUS, in a house that nearly burned to the ground our freshman year, a result of that perennial college miscalculation: tapestry-to-lighter proximity. Now it is a patchwork of turn-of-the-last-century wooden floorboards and contemporary parquet; dusty striped wallpaper in one room, newly spackled walls in another. As we approach from down the street, we can see a black light glowing blue in one of the upstairs windows.

Taline is going as "businesswoman at holiday party." Her costume consists of a thrifted hot-pink power suit and nude pumps. Her hair is pulled up into a chignon—uncharacteristic, for it to be out of her face. The "holiday party" will come as the night progresses, one drink at a time.

I am a birthday candle. It was never a curse for me, being born on Halloween, not like it is for the kids who share their special day with Jesus. It's as if everyone is celebrating me while I get to be someone else. I have a swath of white cotton wound around my body, approximating a wax swirl, and atop my head, a wild whoosh of flames, constructed by Taline out of wire, gold lamé, and sparkling red, orange, and yellow netting. The crown is secured to my ponytail with three hallmates' worth of bobby pins. The metallic glitter on my eyelids periodically floats down into my contact lenses: sharp, glinting pain.

We pause outside the house so I can crouch down and peer into a parked car's side-view mirror to fish an errant sparkle from my eyeball. I catch it on my pinkie tip.

"Make a wish, Valerie," Taline says before she blows it off into the night. The street smells of sweet leaf rot. "What did you wish for?" she asks, and I say, "You blew too fast. I didn't have a chance." We snort with laughter. What a lie—I wished for what I always do: Elliot Thomas. The party is at his house. He's our age but took a gap year, so is a class below us. He is the most aloof human being on earth, as far as I can tell. He's tall, prone to slouching; who knows what his hair is like under his constant black knit cap. Eye contact with him is a spine tingle, is fleeting, is the awe of crushing a firefly in your palm, of thinking: This is magical, I am powerful, oh and now it's dead.

Ahead of us on the sidewalk is a parade of flesh punctuated by small stitches of fabric. One girl wears only a French flag and a beret. There's a nurse whose ass I can see from all the way back here, taut and spliced by a red thong. Meanwhile, I'm in a full bedsheet, which I'd thought suggestive. But these girls up ahead, they skip the suggestion and go straight to the statement.

I smooth my swath around my hips, nod a "now or never" at Taline and suddenly there is a cold, exploding pain at my temple. My first thought is the glitter, but then something oozes—I feel a dripping, a pooling, in my ear, at my collarbone. My second thought is blood. The blow was hard. Have I been shot?

Taline kicks at the retreating car with such furor that her pump flies off into a pile of raked leaves. "Assholes!" she shouts.

My hand comes away from my head sticky with clear, viscous goo. I wipe more of it from my crown, my hair, my eyebrow. Yellow.

"I've been egged?"

Tal chews her bottom lip.

"You can laugh," I say, and she does. I help her find her shoe.

She is peeling wet leaves from her stockinged foot when I say, "I hope you'll still go?"

"Alone?" she says. "Who do you think you're dealing with here?"

*

We are halfway back to campus, consoling ourselves that joining our hallmates' J-horror movie marathon will be just as fun, when, there in front of us, is Elliot. He's got a case of beer under his arm; forgoing the knit cap, he has a plastic axe lodged in his head, blood clotting his long, dark hair (!) and smeared across his forehead. He's with Tova and Desmond, who carry more beer.

"Val and Tal," Des says.

We say hi. We don't mind the rhyme: Val and Tal or, less often, but occasionally, Tal and Val. Although we don't look very much alike, we get mistaken for each other when we're apart. We answer to each other's name. People are confused when we're not together—people including us. *Where's your other half?* they say, and we look around, wondering, too.

Des continues: "You're going the wrong way."

"Nice shoulder pads," Tova says to Taline. Taline shimmies them in thanks.

"We're going to watch a movie," I say, tilting my head so that the good side is pointed toward them.

"Ridic," Tova says. "You've got the rest of your life for movies. Help me carry this beer." She deposits her box on the ground, tears open the top, and hands me two six-packs. Her whole face is painted white: eyelashes, eyelids, lips, and freckles. Her nails, too. I take the beer, and she kisses me on the lips. Whatever drug they're on has made two out of the three of them extra friendly. My red lipstick leaves a smudge on her mouth.

Elliot is trudging ahead, not waiting for our faux protest.

"You have egg on your face," Des says. "Is that conceptual? Are you idioms?"

"I'm an English major," I say. "I should have thought of that. It was some townies."

Taline gives me a Look and I apologize. We don't say words like that. We've gone to community building meetings.

"Come get cleaned up," Tova says, and Des puts his arm around Taline's shoulders, poking his fingers into her football-player '80s hulk. We about-face.

Inside the house, where the party has started even though we're arriving with the hosts, a group composed of the semi-naked women we'd seen earlier and a cohort of Elliot, Tova, and

Des's goth friends cheer when the beer appears. A Freudian Slip and an Oxford Comma—she in an actual silky slip, he in the eponymous shoes and a punctuated T-shirt—are already making out against the wall. "English majors," mutters Taline, who used to be one, too, until she switched to fine art this semester.

I take a sip of warm beer, grab Elliot's arm, and say, "Show me your bathroom?" as if I need him to find it. He hardly acknowledges having heard me, yet places his hand—his fingers, really—on my lower back and steers me toward the hall. The egg is drying on my face, pulling at my skin. In the cloudy bathroom mirror, it looks plastic and shiny.

"Are you a match?" he asks. The question indicates that, at some point in the last fifteen minutes, he has noticed me. My eyes have hardly left him—how could I not have seen it? I must have been distracted by all the puns.

I flick a piece of shell—brown, which is surprising—from my hairline. "Guess again," I say. He leans in the doorway, doesn't. The fact that he hasn't left yet is a marvel. "It's my birthday," I say. "That's your clue."

"Twenty-one?" he asks.

I nod, dabbing my face with a damp tissue. I want to remove egg, retain glitter.

"Every mistress in every movie, right? Always twenty-one." He straightens up. Is he leaving?

"Except when they're twenty-two, or maybe twenty-six," I say, trying to untangle his thought process. Does he picture me as someone who could be a mistress? And is that good or bad? "I'm a birthday candle."

He takes my shoulders in his large hands, leans forward, his lips formed into an O. Here it is, I think—I die at twenty-one. He blows.

"Did you make a wish?" I ask. But he's already gone.

*

Wadded-up toilet paper takes the egg off of my skin, but there's no good way to get it out of my hair without unpinning my flames, and I can't bear to do that after all the time it took to get them affixed and upright. I press the bruise blooming on my temple, watching it pale, then flood back blue, and hope I can make it through the night before anything starts to rot.

I exit the bathroom and Tova grabs me around the waist, holding a beer bottle to my mouth and tipping it up like she's feeding a baby. "Do you know what I am?" she asks. I would answer but she won't move the bottle. I try to indicate my assent. "What?" she keeps saying. "What?"

Des calls her away to the kitchen. I swallow the last of her beer, sputtering and searching for Taline. Most everyone has gathered in what, if this were a normal house, would be the living room. Here it is a sort of museum of failed technology: a bulbous television screen encased in a wooden cabinet, a Commodore 64 with its insides missing, a transistor radio spray-painted yellow, and a record player propped up on a stack of old *National Geographic*s playing "Monster Mash" at the wrong speed. The thong girls and the conceptual kids—and Elliot—sit in a circle in the middle of a faded Persian rug and spin an empty beer bottle among them. It seems early for this sort of game—or late, since the last time I saw it played was in seventh grade—but there they are, crawling on all fours to meet in the middle. They're strangely businesslike about it, spinning, kissing, retreating, and spinning again. I exert great force of will to remain deadpan as Elliot sucks the Freudian Slip's lower lip. I can't get over his long hair.

Taline is in the dark stairwell, sipping from a paper cup full of vodka. Her pumps are on the step beside her.

"I think I have a headache," I say.

"Projectiles will do that to you," she says.

I test my bruise again: still hurts. "You should have let me go home."

"We aren't leaving until my costume is complete," she says, tossing back the rest of her drink, a lock of hair liberating itself from her updo. I stop myself from saying how pretty she looks with her hair back, even though it's true. I don't want to sound like her mother. I pull her to her feet.

Tova and Des have wiggled into the game and won't let us pass by to get more drinks. "Sit *down*," they say.

I keep going, but Des grabs my calf and pinches it, trying to pull me down next to him. I yelp. Taline shrugs and sits. I would rather never kiss Elliot than kiss him under these cir-cumstances. I feign acquiescence, but the instant I hit the rug, I tuck my knees and roll out of Des's grasp, roll again, and clamber back to my feet.

Taline is dying laughing. Des says, "Eggcellent."

Alone in the kitchen, I find a tray of Jell-O shots that haven't set. I slurp a neon green one and it burns going down. I am transfixed by a shiny beige phone sitting in a cradle, the parts connected by a spiral cord. A rotary. I lift it to my ear, fit my pinkie into the zero, and dial.

Tova and Dès are the collectors, the eccentrics. Elliot would have to reveal an interest in something if he were to add to their reliquary and, as far as I know, that's not a thing he would ever do. We met last year in a women's studies class, which one might think would say something about a person—a young man enrolling in what is still, in the late twentieth century at a progressive liberal arts college, a course primarily populated by women. And, of course, it does say something about him, but it is hard to get a handle on what, exactly. I caught his eye on the first day while this senior—a senior and just getting around to her first women's studies class!—prattled on about how she was there to understand why girls don't have to do pull-ups in gym—which is a fine concern, but not when it is the central concern or injustice in one's life. Seeing my vitriol mirrored in his eyes was a shock to the system. Over the course of the semester, Elliot was studious but quiet, contributing an occasional remark about how our usage of the word "queer" seemed to be "anti-metaphysical," which is a concept I really latched on to, and I know I saw him nod the time I said it might be useful for us to say we "believed in feminisms" rather than "were feminists," because stating what we were meant defining what others were not and ran the risk of setting up an exclusionary system of false binaries. Basically, it was our mutual dislike of our classmates' cheery language of empowerment and our extreme pretension that made it okay for me—or me and Taline—to start hanging around him. We barely ever speak to each other; we speak around each other. Yet I still hold out hope for some kind of heteronormative love story.

It's only when Elliot asks if I'm making a call that I realize I am still holding the phone to my ear. I hang up. "How's the game?" I ask, watching his Adam's apple as he knocks back a cherry shot.

"Devolved," he says. "Too much giggling. You want to go fuck up those people who egged you?" He's not even looking at me but at his own hands, so I can't gauge if he's joking. He's got to be joking.

I open their refrigerator and find it full: kale, orange juice, English muffins, half a purple onion, and a tub of vanilla yogurt. It's like real people live here. I hold up a carton. "An egg for an egg?"

He adjusts his bloody axe, gathering his long hair in a rubber band he pulls off his wrist. I blink, trying both not to comment on his hair and to force an errant piece of glitter from my field of vision. It doesn't work. I bat a celestial gaze.

On the way out, I want to catch Taline's eye with my starry one, but she's got hers closed, and is making out with the girl in the flag. Maybe we'll both have a good night.

*

Outside the sky is completely clear, the air just cold enough to sharpen my senses. I don't feel drunk except in the knowledge that Elliot asked me to escape the party with him. We pick our way over the piles of waterlogged leaves and discarded beer cans littering the path from the house to the sidewalk and start to walk. After a block or two, his hand is on my back, on a place where my bedsheet lets slip a bit of skin. He runs his finger back and forth on this invisible line of my undoing.

When we stop, we are beyond the regular loop of streets where most of the off-campus housing is. Nobody trick-or-treats around here. The streetlights are fewer and farther between; the houses are both bigger and more run-down. There's a stone wall around one that, despite being in shambles, is a mansion of sorts. When this was an industrial boomtown, some baron probably lived there. Elliot places the egg carton on the wall, careful not to let it fall. He slouches against the crumbling stone. I stay on the sidewalk.

His eyes are on me, like he's waiting for me to say or do something. If he were someone else, I see what I could do. The way he's leaning there against the wall, I could get closer. I could fit my leg between his, match my body to his, and lean into him, too. It's almost like I could do that, almost. I know how to flirt, how to go home with someone or bring them home with me. First semester of college, I learned how to craft an essay, and how to do that. But I've never wanted a person so much. If I miscalculate, misalign, misread, I think I'll go up in flames. "I don't know how to get back to the party from here," I say.

"Do you want to go back?" he asks with this small, crooked smile on his face. I feel like I've never seen him smile before. I shake my head no and he says, "Me neither." I take the smallest step closer to him and he reaches out a hand, encircles my wrist, and pulls. We are face-to-face. He still has a plastic axe lodged in his hair. We are not kissing. Not yet.

But we are just about to when, behind me, a car backs up. I hear it, and then I see Elliot go for the eggs. He takes two and

I think he's going to hand me one, but instead he tosses them, one after the other. I hear them hit: a crack and a splash, a crack and a splash. Elliot is not just smiling now but laughing. I still don't turn around because I don't want to leave the moment when it is just us, when something is about to happen. I don't want to see what is actually happening because what I hear next sounds like two car doors.

Then I'm pushed aside, and I land hard on the sidewalk. My sheet tears; gravel bites my leg. In front of me, the first punch is hard to discern—it's dark and Elliot is already covered in fake blood. Is there more blood now? And then—there's no denying that there is. Swinging wildly are two guys in makeshift costumes, one wearing that white distorted horror movie mask and the other the classic hockey mask. I know I'm screaming, but no one is coming to save us. To save him. I scramble to my feet. They shove me away so easily. Elliot is on the ground, and they aren't letting up. The axe falls into the dirt and the hockey guy stomps on it. With a pop, it bursts, splitting down the middle seam, deflating into an unrecognizable piece of trash. What if they stomp on him like that? Elliot gets a grip on the movie mask guy's pants and pulls. Amid the shouting—we are all shouting—I hear the ping of the button at his fly hitting the street. He's wearing boxers with kissy-faces on them. Who bought those for him? What would she think of this? He has to hold up his pants with one hand now, so I try again, grabbing on to him and tugging, trying to pull him away. His arm is cold, with no give to it. He shakes me off like I'm nothing and swings as Elliot struggles to his feet. When his fist connects with Elliot's face, it's a sound like the egg hitting the car.

What can I do but run for help at the closest house, and then, when no one opens the door, the next, and the next? By the time someone answers, understands me through my hysterics, and calls for help, by the time that happens, I'm not sure which direction I came from. I'm not sure which way to point.

*

I call his house all night. Finally, finally, Tova answers. His face, she says—he needed surgery. For some of the rest of it, his ribs and all the bruises, they'll just have to wait. She says he is not okay, not now, but the doctors say he will be. She says no, I cannot come to see him. She doesn't say more; she hangs up the phone. I blink as if, when I open my eyes, I'll be back in that one starlit moment. I blink, and when I open my eyes, it is morning. I blink, and when I open my eyes, it is November.

POINTS OF LIGHT
Taline, 2000

WHEN I STEP INTO THE ART STUDIO, the first thing I see are breasts. The air is so redolent with paint thinner, I can taste it at the back of my throat. I don't know what I thought "life painting" meant when I registered for the summer course at the community college near my mom's house, but I wasn't expecting nudity. The model has assumed a very casual pose on a platform at the center of the room, with her weight settled on one foot and her arms crossed loosely at the waist. She has long, dark hair pulled back into a braid and those small, upturned, pink-nippled breasts. It's not that I have a problem with them. They're great. Nudity is fine. I'm fine. How cool that she's comfortable with her body. It's just that I could never.

What maybe I have a problem with is everyone else in the class. It's a lot of adults—not my kind of twenty-year-old adult but people in their forties, fifties, and sixties. How late am I that they already seem to have works in progress? I'm always late when I have to rely on my mother for a ride and today is no exception. But have I really missed all the introductions, the instructions, the preamble? I'm already supposed to know how to do this?

I skirt the perimeter of the space and find an open easel. I prop up my blank canvas, making a wall between myself and the rest of the room. I take my time squirting an array of paints onto my palette and pour my own tiny pungent cup of paint thinner. There's light conversation in the air, maybe between friends who registered for the class together, but no authoritative voice rings out. I wonder if there's no teacher at all until a woman wearing cat-eye glasses and a paint-flecked apron tied around her heavily pregnant belly appears at my side. She introduces herself as Bess, then loops an arm around my waist and moves me a foot to the side. "You have to angle yourself so you can see both your canvas and the model at the same time," she says. I nod. I could have figured that out myself if a direct view of the model was what I was after. I wait for her to tell me more, to tell me what to do, but once she's satisfied with my stance, she moves on. This is all very different from my usual art courses at school, not that I've had that many of them. I switched majors late in the game—junior year—and need this summer credit to graduate on time.

I peer at the model, dip a brush in paint, and poke at my canvas. Maybe beginning with her head will be easier than trying to get her whole body into this first painting. I start at the top, at the part in her hair, then use my rag—an old pillowcase I found in the back of the linen closet—to scratch out what I've done. I try again and again, but my vantage point is too weird. I hadn't considered that when picking my spot in the room. Faces have a strange topography, it turns out, when viewed from three-quarters of the way to the back. What would my chin look like from this angle? I've never inspected an ear from behind before, or noticed that a forehead isn't a clean slope. I slip my fingers underneath my bangs and confirm: weird. I shake my hair back into place.

When Bess's kitchen timer rings to signal the model's break, I'm startled and jerk my arm across the canvas in a single, assured line—the only real line on the whole white plane. The model stretches and ties her robe. The students begin to rotate through the room, sneaking glances at each other's work. They're mostly retirees, probably, and middle-aged mommies getting some me-time. The one guy who seems to be my age makes his way over.

He smells of smoke and sweat—like, strongly, as if he hasn't washed his shirt in a few weeks. It's a fog around him, making his presence truly impossible to ignore. But I do ignore him, fumbling around in my bag as if I'm searching for something. There is nothing appealing to me about talking to a guy from my hometown, or a town adjacent to my hometown. I had to do that for long enough and now I'm over it. He's looking at my painting, which is basically nothing, a blank canvas cut through with a line or two. If anything, he should be the one to say something, since he is the one who walked across the room. When I can't avoid him any longer, I stop fiddling with the top of my water bottle, which I've been screwing and unscrewing, and meet his eyes. They're the color of the yellow ochre paint on my palette. He has the kind of bad skin that probably would be fine if he washed his hair more.

"I'm Kyle," he says.

After a beat, I say, "Taline."

"What kind of name is that?" he asks.

"Armenian," I say. He nods, as if that means anything to him. "What kind of name is Kyle?" The timer rings and everyone returns to their spots. I watch them get right back to work. I watch and watch. At the end of class, I shove my blank canvas into my assigned slot in the drying rack and hustle out the door.

*

That evening, my thoughts are caught in a loop. I call Val and ask her what she thinks my problem was.

"You've internalized the male gaze," she says. She sounds authoritative, but what if I'm just a bad artist?

Last summer, I bruised a belt around my middle with obsessive hula-hooping, trying to trim down my hips. I'd gotten the idea on a visit to an art museum, where I'd seen a video of an artist named Sigalit Landau hula-hooping with barbed wire. It was mesmerizing, watching the abrasions form on her smooth, nude skin, their color deepening with each revolution. I remember reading the label after and finding out that the piece was about borders. Her body was the only home she felt she had. I'd been so embarrassed that it was the flatness of her stomach that had captured my attention first, not the deep personal and political conflict reflected in the piece.

I'd been embarrassed, but not embarrassed enough to stop myself from finding my old Hula-Hoop when I got home from the city. My childhood best friend, Zoe, not one to consider the implications of the male gaze, had once reached out and given a hard pinch to the roll of my stomach above my waistband. This was when we were fourteen or so. She probably forgot about it five seconds after she did it; I've felt the sharp surprise of it every single day since. I loved the meditative aspect of the hula-hooping but didn't keep it up after the bruises started to accumulate.

Sigalit Landau didn't have problems committing to her artwork. She was ready to scar herself for it. After my mother retreats to her room for the night, I slip out of the house and lift the hoop down from the hook it hangs on in the garage. I stay out until midnight, the hoop orbiting me, until I can't catch my breath.

*

I'm nearly twenty minutes late to the second week of painting class. Arriving at the door and seeing everyone's paintings in progress—full bodies sketched out on their canvasses, shading going in, and highlights picking up—makes me feel like I shouldn't even bother. But my goal for this week, the one I've set in my head, is merely to get something down on the canvas that's recognizable as part of a woman—a foot, a nose, anything. The same model from last week is there on the platform, perched on the edge of a stool.

Bess gestures me over to an open easel that happens to be right next to Kyle. "I was afraid you weren't coming back," she says. "I always take it personally when students drop the class."

"Sorry I'm late," I say. "My mom forgot she needed to drive me."

I position my canvas and squirt out a rainbow of paint, most of which I'll probably waste. Then I sit down on my stool, considering my first move. I'm at a better angle this week.

I can smell Kyle just as clearly today. Is his shirt the same one? I think it is. I pick a flat brush and rinse it in mineral spirits, then thin out a bit of paint. I make a random mark on the canvas to see how it looks. I work on the same canvas I used last week, which despite its three hours of prior service, remains blank. I make a few more slashes and dashes across the surface before lifting my head to look at the model's actual form.

I'm holding my paintbrush, poised to do *something*, when Kyle asks, "No car?"

I shake my head.

"Where do you live?" he asks. His shoulders are rounded toward his easel, his chest concave, his hair hanging down over his face. I'm sitting in the exact same way. I hesitate but straighten up and give him the intersection.

"Yeah, I know it," he says. "I'll drive you next week. Pick you up at five fifteen."

I don't necessarily want him to drive me, but it would be easier to have a ride that's not my mother. She's happy to have me here for the summer, but she's got her own life and it's not her fault that I never learned to drive. Or, it *is* her fault—she was the one who tried to teach me, but I could never relax into learning with her constant screeches and "oh Gods" as I eased my foot onto the gas pedal. "Okay," I tell him. "Thanks."

I get lost for a moment, watching him paint. He's doing something strange with the proportions of the figure, elongating her neck and torso, making her head smaller. He paints like he's drawing, outlining the features of her face, the bone of her clavicle, and the curve under her breasts. If I could do that, maybe I wouldn't care how I smelled either.

I retrain my focus on the model. I look for a shape, any shape, I think I can reproduce. At the end of class, when I step back to assess my work, it looks like it was done by one of those painting elephants. I dip my rag in mineral spirits and wipe the canvas clean.

*

Kyle picks me up in a cloud of pot smoke. The car is practically hotboxed. "This doesn't feel safe," I say to him.

"I'm a better driver when I'm high," he says. He holds out a joint. I take it because I'd rather I be smoking it than him, and also because maybe it wouldn't hurt to loosen up a little.

As we drive, he tells me that he works at the art supply store over on the highway and gets a 50 percent discount when he shops there. He's a student at the community college and is taking the painting course for credit, too.

"You're a really good artist," I say, flipping down the passenger seat visor. As I do, a flurry of traffic tickets falls into my lap.

"I'd return the compliment, but I don't think you've painted anything yet?" he says. "Is someone making you take this class?"

"Kind of," I say. "I switched majors late and didn't have time during the regular year for all the requirements." My eyes are red. I take one more pull and hand the joint back to him as we turn into the parking lot, glad to have made it in one piece. I am not sure if I'm being paranoid or if all the adults exchange looks when we go in together.

I can do this, I think to myself. I start to dab paint. I draw a middle line to correspond with the model's spine, showing the curve of her body, the lean of her ribs, and the stretch of her neck. I peer around my canvas at the model. Is Hank, the older man across the room, looking at me? I turn to ask Kyle if he thinks so, but Kyle is looking at me, too. It dawns on me that Valerie was actually right—like totally, incredibly right. My thighs are sticking to the stool in the summer heat. I wish I wasn't wearing a sundress. I stand and feel a little more covered up. Kyle gestures at my canvas, and I start painting again.

Bess circles the room and, as she swings by us, says, "Interesting tactic, you two." I want to die.

"At least she's painting," Kyle says.

Bess nods. "Watch her arms," she says. "You don't want to give her T. rex arms."

Kyle bats his arms around, elbows at his side, and I see what she means. They're too short. I scratch them out and try again.

When I was little, my drawings were always the ones picked to go on the bulletin board at school. My teachers went wild for them. Should I not have taken any of that seriously?

"Don't do it!" Kyle says when he sees me poised with the rag, but I can't help it. I scrub.

*

The next week, I'm on the fence until Kyle pulls up. He's high again. I lean in the window and say, "I'm dropping the class. Tell Bess for me?" He makes a half-hearted attempt to convince me to get in the car, but I stand firm, and he drives off. When I call the school to ask for a refund, though, they tell me I'd have had to withdraw two sessions earlier to qualify for that. And I do need the credit, so what choice do I have but to go back? The following week, I realize Kyle's not coming to pick me up and my mom is busy, so I call Zoe to drive me before her shift at the scoop shop she's working at this summer. I climb into her car and she says, "You gotta get over this driving thing."

"I know," I say.

"I'd swap places and let you practice, but I need my car. Don't want you crashing it or something." She pulls away from the curb and turns up the music. It's a CD I remember us going to get together when we were freshmen in high school. She sings along. I resist for a few blocks. I haven't listened to this band in ages. Dude-fronted jam bands are so not my thing anymore. They weren't my thing then, either, but if I wanted a social life in high school, I didn't really have a choice but to listen to them. Although I'd like to say I don't remember all of the words, I do. By the time we pull up to the art center, we've got the windows rolled down and we're harmonizing just how we used to, cracking ourselves up with our terrible voices.

"I'm not picking you up," Zoe says, winking.

*

When I walk through the classroom door, I'm unmoored. The model's platform is empty and in a slightly different spot on the floor. And where is Bess?

A stocky man with splatter-stained construction boots, canvas pants, and a ponytail approaches me. "Can I help you?"

"No," I say, stepping back.

"I mean," he continues, "are you in this class? I haven't seen you."

"Are *you* in this class?" I ask.

"I teach it," he says, holding out his hand. "Jeremiah."

"What about Bess?" I say, realizing where she is the moment the question leaves my mouth. "Did she have a boy or girl?"

Jeremiah seems surprised by the question. "I didn't ask," he says.

Pulling out my canvas from last class, I can see the ghost of what I'd painted before. The arms are still too short, but it isn't as bad as I remember. Kyle drags his easel over next to me. "You shouldn't have erased it," he says.

"They wouldn't refund me for the class," I answer.

Jeremiah has an entirely different style from Bess. He asks everyone to start off by painting their canvas with a wash of brown. I don't really know what that means. I glance around the room—Kyle's messing with the hem of his shirt, but everyone else is dousing their canvases in a wet, translucent layer of paint, so I do, too. It seems like a good start; my disappointing painting from last time disappears under the veil of burnt umber.

It isn't until my canvas is fully covered that the model finally arrives. I hear Jeremiah say, "You know the class started ten minutes ago, right?" She apologizes, climbs onto the platform, and drops her robe.

"Now," Jeremiah says, "grab your rags and dip them in your mineral spirits. What I want you to do is look for the planes of light on her body. Remove the ground of paint where you see that light."

I am so relieved to have directions to follow. It's like finger-painting. I pick up the light on the model's forehead, her little nose, the tops of her shoulders, and her clavicle. "Good," Jeremiah says when he circles by. I feel that rush that comes with validation. Despite myself, it is coupled with relief. He grabs the canvas off my easel and heads across the room with it. When he's back against the opposite wall, he holds it up and yells, "See her?"

I do.

*

The next week, Kyle is back to pick me up. The car is conspicuously smoke-free. He says, "I'm trying something new."

"I noticed something was different," I say. Outside, I see a tree with red in its leaves. I'm looking forward to going back to campus for senior year. High school conditioned into me a fear of the fall, that red portends the end of summer, but now it means I'll get to be on campus, with Val and our other friends again. Should I be friends with Kyle? It seems like he stopped smoking in the car for me. "What do you think of Jeremiah?" I ask. "The new teacher?"

Kyle brakes for what seems like an interminable amount of time at a stop sign. "I heard him tell one of the mommies that he's twenty-nine. He's, like, barely older than I am. I don't trust the dude," he says. "He's got control issues, I think—he's always got these instructions."

"I mean, he is our teacher," I say. "So the instruction thing doesn't seem too problematic."

Kyle glances over at me. "You into him or something?"

"Yeah, I totally want to fuck him," I say. When he turns red, I'm glad that I made him feel uncomfortable. That he might be right is beside the point. There's a pause where neither of us says anything, and then it's like we both decide to laugh. It's easier that way.

*

In class, Jeremiah does, in fact, have more directions for us. He walks around the room greeting everyone. He's barely taller than I am, but he's built like a block and seems bigger than he is. The ponytail may help with that—it gives him a presence. He touches my elbow as he says hello and his eyes, I notice, seem to linger on the space where my collar hangs away from my body, where a person, if he were looking, could see a little way down my shirt. I feel Jeremiah's heat on my elbow long after he's moved on to the other side of the room.

Kyle and I set up our easels to the rear of the still vacant model's stand, and Jeremiah announces that he'd like us to prepare our canvases with a wash of color, right over what we'd been doing last week, to create more depth and dimension. Then he'd like us to mix some blue with the brown on our palettes and lay in shadows to contrast the highlights. I dive in with ultramarine. Kyle stands and stews, his canvas white. If I had a style already, a real voice in my work, maybe I'd feel the same way, but to me it seems arrogant for Kyle to think he's got nothing to learn from Jeremiah.

The model finally arrives. She's dressed in street clothes rather than her typical robe: tight jeans, a gauzy tunic with a blue blazer over it—a strange combination—and high-heeled boots. Jeremiah heads over to her and seems to voice a quiet complaint at her lateness. She's flustered as she takes to the stand and starts to disrobe. Seeing her undress from her street clothes is particularly strange. Part of what I've been doing the last few weeks, I realize, is retraining my own gaze: trying to divorce the sight of a naked body here in art class from all the associations I have with one in other contexts. Last week, as I pulled out the highlights and blocked in the shadows, I was able to see her as tones and shades, planes and angles. I didn't see breasts or belly, cellulite or down, just volume and value. I wasn't thinking about my own thighs. I wasn't thinking about sex. When she's unclasping her peachy cotton bra behind her back and peeling off her thong right in front of us, that becomes much harder to do. Watching her underwear turn inside out as she slides it down past her knees, I feel like I'm unwittingly breaking a contract.

I pull over a stool and sit on it so my view is blocked by my canvas. Kyle watches her, though. He sees me noticing and twitches but doesn't look away.

Jeremiah passes by when we're halfway through class. I'm excited, wondering if he's going to pick up my canvas again and show me that I'm doing a good job. I want to see what the painting looks like from across the room. "You know," he says to me, "I think you'd be able to see better if you didn't do that with your hair."

I stiffen. This is the kind of thing my mother says to me. My bangs are in my face; they always are. Now, though, it's like I can feel each strand against my skin. "I can see fine," I say.

"Maybe," Jeremiah says, leaning in closer, touching my shoulder. "But I think you could see better than fine if you didn't do that. No one here is looking at you."

I can tell that Kyle is listening. It's preposterous to say that no one is looking. Jeremiah's looking. Kyle is. Across the room, Hank is. I wait for Jeremiah to move on and, finally, he does.

*

The next week, the class sits in front of their easels, puttering around with their palette knives and paints, while Jeremiah paces the length of the studio. The model is nowhere to be found. Ten minutes go by, then fifteen. Jeremiah has us sketch studies of our own feet. "Kahlo and Basquiat both famously learned to paint by drawing their own feet," he says. Then, "Jesus Christ. Okay, everyone."

I'm confused as he walks toward me, briskly and with purpose. I shrink back as he extends his hand and takes my elbow. He ushers me toward the platform in the middle of the room. I dig my heels in like a petulant toddler, pulling back his arm.

"What are you doing?" I whisper.

He turns to face me, and everyone is watching—the mommies, Hank, Kyle. "Obviously I'm not asking you to take your clothes off," he says, quietly enough that only I can hear him. This makes it worse, somehow, that we're whispering. I'm blushing so hard I can see that even my chest is red. I curse myself for leaving that one extra button undone.

I feel dizzy with terror. Every particle of charcoal dust in the air seems to gather in my eyes.

"Hey, man," Kyle pipes up from behind me. "She doesn't want to do it."

An excruciating moment passes before I feel Jeremiah's hand drop from my arm. "Fine," he says. "You want to do it, *man*? Or is class canceled?"

A groan spreads through the room. I feel responsible.

"Taline," Kyle says. "Just walk away."

The unflinching way he's looking at Jeremiah is scary. He's taller than Jeremiah but much scrawnier. His hand is clenched into a fist, and I can only imagine how Jeremiah would crush him if he tried to throw a punch. I know I'm the excuse for this display, not the cause of it. Kyle's wanted to challenge Jeremiah ever since he walked into the room.

Not that anyone else knows that. It looks to them, I'm sure, that Kyle is up here like a jackass, defending my honor. I've never felt so conspicuous and yet so invisible at the same time. Standing between the two of them, in the middle of a roomful of people staring at me, stepping up onto the model's platform becomes, somehow, the only way out.

"Whatever," I say. "It's fine."

I might as well be at the top of a skyscraper, the way my vision narrows and my breathing grows shallow. I lean against the stool, ankles crossed and arms folded.

Jeremiah snaps out of his staring contest with Kyle and joins me. He grips my shoulders and angles my upper body to the left. I suck in my stomach as far as it will go. I feel like I might die when he brushes my hair to the side. I shake it back into place, but still he steps down from the stand, satisfied.

Everyone starts to work, many of them swapping out their paintings of the model for fresh canvases or pieces of paper. Kyle's mouth is set in a line. I half expect him to gather his things and leave, but after a minute or two, he also grabs a new canvas and gets started. What is he going to do to me? I can't watch him work even though I've stupidly positioned myself—or allowed myself to be positioned—facing him. I train my eyes out the window, at the fork in a tree branch, focusing on how it seems to shiver whenever a car passes by.

"Pay particular notice," I hear Jeremiah say, "to the swoop of her collarbone, how it is in tension with her shoulders. Do you see that?"

A few moments later, he says to someone standing behind me, "I like how you've delineated her spine, how it runs down under her shirt."

I've never been so aware of these parts of my body. As he talks, it's as if Jeremiah's there with his brush, painting them onto me. I feel all the places he touched, with his hands or his attention. Did I have shoulders before? A spine?

I think he's doing it on purpose, making me feel this way. Part of me is furious. I'm here to paint; I'm not here for this. But it would be a lie to say that I don't kind of like it.

Jeremiah circulates through the room, nodding and offering suggestions as he moves. He pauses in front of me and leans on the platform. Under normal circumstances, if he looked at me for this long, I would shift my eyes; I would laugh and turn away. But I can't ruin everyone's paintings. I hold still and I hold his gaze. "You okay?" he asks. I am.

*

When class ends and I'm released from my modeling duties, I step off the platform. My body realigns but doesn't quite relax. Some of the mommies turn their canvases to show me what they've done. It is kind of neat to see all these versions of myself, but I don't want to look too closely. What if there's something there I don't want to see?

I hustle over to my unused art supplies and shove them into my bag. Jeremiah strides up to me and says, "Thanks for doing that."

Kyle is at my side before I can respond. "We gotta go," he says.

"You have to show her your painting," Jeremiah says. "It's your best work so far."

"You've known me three weeks," Kyle says.

"It looks like there's real feeling behind it," Jeremiah presses. He is being such an asshole, teasing Kyle like that. I should stick up for him, or just walk out with him, but I can't make myself.

Kyle looks between me and Jeremiah one more time, and then he leaves.

"He was my ride," I say. For a second, I consider running after him.

"I'll drive you," Jeremiah says. "Traffic back to Brooklyn is always better when I go home a little later anyway."

"You live in Brooklyn?" I ask as he rinses his hands in the perpetually clogged sink and dries them on his jeans. He does dress like he lives in New York City. Jeremiah, until this moment, had been contained only in this room, in this art studio, but of course his world is much bigger than that. "Why do you work here?"

"Well," he says, "the drive's not too bad, actually. I haven't finished my MFA yet, but they still hired me, which is cool. And I like it. It's interesting."

I follow him out to the parking lot. "You think this job is interesting?"

"I do," he says. "The people in it are so random—like, Helen is a hair colorist and Lila is an oncologist. Hank used to be in the Marines. It's just fascinating, I think, to see these people who've chosen different paths but still want to devote part of their week to making art."

"Kyle and I just call all those women 'mommies,'" I say. "I never really thought about them. Or Hank."

"You and Kyle," he says, "are a little less interesting to me."

"Hey," I say.

"Joking. You *are* interesting, actually," he says, although his only potential basis for finding me interesting is that I've left my shirt unbuttoned a little too far.

We get to his car, an enormous beat-up boat that looks like it could have been an airport limo in its last life. When I was little, it used to be the highlight of family vacations, getting picked up in a black town car to be taken to the airport. That, and the airport dogs. I hardly needed the actual vacation. The backseat of Jeremiah's car is littered with stretchers, a roll of canvas, and a teetering stack of library books.

"That's a lot of books," I say.

"School," he says. "You know." He pops open the back door so we can see them better.

I point at the one on top, about Arshile Gorky. "He was Armenian," I say. "My relatives always bring him up when they hear I'm an art major. His paintings look like they're of my cousins."

Jeremiah picks up the book and flips through. He finds a portrait of a young woman and holds it up next to my face. "I see the resemblance," he says. Then he grabs the book that was under the Gorky. "Oh—let me show you this one. Lucian Freud. You know him?"

I don't. He opens it to an image of a painting: a woman on a bed, her limbs strewn across the blue-white sheets like someone in the deep abandon of sleep.

"I don't paint a lot of nudes," Jeremiah says. "But when I got hired to teach here, I thought I'd try to use it as a learning experience, too. Freud paints from the inside out." He runs his index finger over the woman's long, bent leg. "See her veins here? He paints the veins, layers the flesh over them, the skin over that. He's like a sculptor."

I squint at the painting. I like it—even this photograph of the painting seems to have texture and depth—but I also find it disturbing. There is something heightened about the nudity. Like, everyone can already see this woman's breasts; does he have to show them her insides, too?

Jeremiah pulls another book from the pile. He closes the car door, leans against it, and gestures for me to do the same.

"Speaking of nudity," he says, handing the book to me. "Do you know Ana Mendieta's work?"

As I leaf through it, I can't decide what I'm looking at.

Are these self-portraits? Landscapes? The same woman, Ana Mendieta, is in them, or if not her, her form, her absence. She's covered in mud or leaves, blending into nature, her impression an angel in a snowbank or a bloodred outline in the dirt. I turn the page again and there she is with hair glued to her face, a sort of uncanny beard. The pictures are funny and unsettling. It's clear to me that she is the one in charge of the images. She's the subject and the one making the picture. Her work is like the antidote to the paintings we were just looking at. I've never seen anything like it before. I want the book. I want to look at it forever. My hands get a familiar itch in them, something that's been latent in class. "She's lighting it all on fire," I say.

Jeremiah raises an eyebrow, then gestures to the car. "Climb on in."

As we pull out of the parking lot, I'm still paging through the book. "I really like this," I say.

"You know what happened to her?" Jeremiah says. "She went out a window. That's what her husband said. He actually was put on trial for killing her. I just saw his sculpture show downtown."

I tighten my grip on the book. "Hey," I say. "Where are we going?"

He's quiet for a second, during which my throat goes dry. Whenever Val or I go home with someone, we make sure the other knows where we'll be. He says, "I wasn't thinking. I just started driving."

In the inky twilight, it takes a moment to get my bearings, but when I tell him where to go, he goes.

"You know," Jeremiah says. "It wasn't fair that I made you model in class today. I mean, you didn't get to paint. That's what you're paying for, right? Let's do a makeup lesson. Can you come back to the studio tomorrow around eight?"

I'm not sure what he's asking me. Is there another class that meets tomorrow, and I'd be joining them? Or—would it just be the two of us? A private session? And if it is that, the second option, would I want that? It would be a great story. I imagine for a second telling Zoe. Then I imagine telling Val. "I don't know," I say, and I don't. When I get out of the car, I take the book.

*

Later, I get into bed with the Ana Mendieta book on my lap. There's this series of photographs I can't stop looking at. They're of her, with a pane of glass pressed up against her face. Her features are contorted, both grotesque and unashamed. I think of how Zoe and I would press our faces on the windows of her parents' car when we were kids. The goal was for someone in another car to see us. That seems like Mendieta's goal, too. *Here I am.* Her body is almost entirely out of the frame, but her shoulders are bare. No makeup. Her eyebrows aren't plucked. She took her beauty and bent it. I run my fingers over the pictures. I can almost see what would have happened if she pressed harder, until the glass cracked, what she would have looked like with the shards splitting her skin. I think I'd picture that even if I didn't know what had happened to her, how she died. It's as if she was dancing right up against danger, against disfigurement. *Here I am.* In her eyes, there was a dare. There still is.

TWENTY-SIX
Valerie, 2004

LOUISE AND I LEAVE THROUGH THE SIDE DOOR. At nearly 9 p.m., our coworkers are still at their desks; it is November 1 tomorrow and we've not yet finalized the rollout of our special holiday merchandise. "Happy birthday, Valerie," everyone joked throughout the day, dropping stack after stack of unrealized requests at my desk. Sure, they also had cupcakes delivered, but we couldn't even take a break long enough to enjoy them. I got cream cheese frosting all over my keyboard.

"If you told me my English degree, let alone my women's studies minor, would be put to use writing puns for a hosiery company . . ." I say as we scramble down fifteen flights of stairs. We couldn't risk running into someone in the elevator who might hand us more work.

"I mean, I actually want to be in fashion," Louise says. "Feminist tights—this is on-brand for me."

I am wearing a pair of those tights right now. As advertised, they don't pinch at the top, which leaves my silhouette love handle–free. They do shred at the toes in mere seconds,

though; a well-kept company secret that I exploit for Halloween purposes once we board the L train and start to assemble
our costumes. I hook an index finger into a burgeoning run and
pull, splitting the fabric to my knee. We tear into the pharmacy
bag we'd filled during a fifteen-minute lunch break, wrapping
Ace bandages around our heads and dabbing navy eye shadow
onto the hollows of our cheeks. I gouge a chunk of red lipstick
from the tube and deposit it at the corner of my mouth. Louise
takes some and rubs it on her teeth.

"That looks evil," I say as she contorts her lips into an un-
holy ghoul's grin. "I love it."

She nods like she agrees but wipes off the lipstick, smudg-
ing the red under her eyes instead. We're in our work clothes
from the neck down: chiffon blouses, pencil skirts, and pumps.
Louise's shirt is powder blue; mine is pink with white dots.
"Dead-end jobs," we clarify when the sweet elderly women
seated across from us ask.

"Another take on the costume," I say as we exit the train in
Brooklyn, "is what would happen to me if you quit."

"We're work wives, Val," Louise says. "I go, you go."

Louise is always threatening to move to a new company.
I believe she believes she can get me a job wherever she winds
up, but who is Louise but a mid-level art director at FreeLove
Tights? Sure, I'm her protégé, her trusty second-in-command,
but it isn't like I work for Bill Gates. I pretend to be anxious
about her impending departure, but the truth is that if she gets
this new job, I won't follow her; I'll quit fashion altogether. The
real, real truth is that I'm going to do it anyway. I just need
another few months.

Out on the street, she follows me. Louise is one of those women for whom the Lower East Side is the be-all and end-all of late night, who thinks that this whole Brooklyn thing will blow over soon. I am the one who lives in Williamsburg and knows where we're going, at least sort of, anyway. Before Taline left the city for grad school last summer, we used to go out around here: to the Polish bar with the giant Styrofoam cups of beer, the club with the glittery wallpaper, and the beer garden that used to be a gas station. We went to parties nearby here, too, but she was usually the one who was invited, often by her summer school art teacher, who would call to tell her about these lofts and gallery openings and goofy happenings she had to come by. Sometimes we'd go and he wouldn't even be there. Tonight, I can find the address we're looking for, I'm pretty sure, but not completely sure. The neighborhood is gentrifying so fast that it is noticeably different every few months.

"Where are the kids?" Louise asks. "I wanted to see some cute kid costumes."

"There are no kids," I say. "Not anymore. Or, not yet." Of course, there are too many people in George W. Bush masks—but they are set off by a fully realized Empire State Building, his spire at least eight feet tall; a sequined mermaid being wheeled in a wagon, her legs bound into an impractical tail; and a perfect cardboard replica of Hokusai's *Great Wave*, complete with small wooden boats rolling down the slope of its wearer's back.

"What do all these people do that they had time to construct these?" Louise says.

"They don't *do* anything," I say.

We head south, where the crowd thins out and Louise grips my arm. I forge ahead, but feel jittery, too. "It's *fine*," I tell her, but how could I not think something bad was about to happen? When I saw the listing for this party in the event pages at the back of a magazine, I clipped it out and stared at it. I carried it around in my pocket, wondering. Halloween. Could I do it? Should I? Ever since what happened with Elliot—to Elliot—my stomach has dropped at the mere mention of Halloween. I called Taline and she said she thought it would be healthy for me to dress up and celebrate again. Halloween was *my* holiday. She might not have said that if I'd told her that what had caught my eye was Des's name in the listing. But I showed the magazine clipping to Louise. She didn't have any more compelling countersuggestions, so we decided yes—we'll go.

We slip through an unmarked gray door into a freight elevator. Louise doesn't believe we're in the right place until we open the metal gate at the sixth floor and peals of disco music shimmer down the dark hall. There is a skeleton at the door with a clipboard; we show our IDs and present our wrists to be stamped. Inside, the party has barely started, but we weren't about to miss the first hour's open bar just to look cool. As nervous as I am, it would be impossible to look cool anyway. We make our way through the room, the air thick with the sweet musk of smoke machine fog, lit by the cosmic sparks off the disco ball. We toast with vodka Red Bulls. "Happy birthday," Louise says. "What is it again?"

"Twenty-six," I say, still no one's mistress, like I wasn't at twenty-one. I touch my temple, wondering, What is Elliot like at twenty-six? I scan the room. Does he still have long hair? "Is it all downhill from here?"

"Yes," she says. I know Louise is a little older than I am, but for some reason I don't dare ask by how much.

We polish off another couple of drinks and watch as people start to venture onto the dance floor, arms bent in their best "Thriller" impressions. I recognize a few of them from around the neighborhood but no one in particular, no one special. Louise and I stand to the side of the bar, dancing a little and trying our best not to seem self-conscious. I feel guilty that this isn't the good time I promised, so I grab her arm and we spiral out into the burgeoning crowd. We start to really dance, and laugh, and maybe have some fun. Then she does a spin and loses a shoe. Is it a sign? I guzzle my drink, shouting into her ear, "Halloween, junior year, my friend Taline lost her shoe."

"And?"

I know I shouldn't jinx anything by talking about that night. If Des is here at this party, if Tova or Elliot is, then they're here. "Taline's in school in Austin and wants me to apply, too! Austen in Austin!"

Louise peers at me from under her Ace bandage, which has slipped down over her right eye, turning her into a zombie pirate. "Would you do that?"

"I mean, no way!" I say, remembering I'm talking to my boss here. With Taline away, I was adrift until I befriended Louise. She was always nice to me, but it was an incremental transition: supervisor to friend. I spill a bit of vodka Red Bull on my shirt. I twirl, jump up and down, and shimmy, trying to distract her from the series of dumb things I've just said aloud. I can't tell her that I've already applied. I can't get excited, or compromise my job, until I get in. But the idea of being with Taline again and throwing myself into exploring this new read—at least I think it's a new read—on *Sense and Sensibility*, well, it's really all I want. Or, almost all I want.

"Your moves aren't nearly as good as his," she says, pointing me toward the new DJ, who announces his takeover of the turntables by executing a high kick over them, his gold four-inch heels reflecting the light from the disco ball.

"Oh!" I cry. I'd worried about how to appear surprised when I saw Des, but his high-glam sort-of drag takes care of that. He *is* here. "Hey, I know him!"

Louise eyes me. "From where?"

"College," I say, carefully dancing us closer to the DJ booth, but behind a pole. I don't want Des to see me, but I want a better look at him. "I had no idea he'd be here . . ."

"I know you're lying but I can't tell why," Louise shouts into my ear. It is much louder now that we're right up next to the speakers. My head thrums with the pulse of the music. I take a few long, slow breaths. Des's makeup looks professional, his eyeliner two perfect metallic wings. His short blond hair is gelled to the side, his body is strong and tan, and he's wearing a fully unbuttoned gold shirt that matches his shoes. He cues up a record, headphones cupped to his ear, and chugs from a bottle of water. The room fills with a song I don't recognize, although Louise and everyone else whoop and cheer for it. I don't know how anyone can keep up—I never know who's singing. I can name more second-wave French feminists than pop stars. I search the crowd. Blue and pink lasers sparkle off the disco ball, refract through the fog, fall on un-familiar faces.

"Aren't you going to talk to him?" Louise asks.

"He wouldn't be happy to see me," I say, knowing it's true when the words leave my mouth. I dance around her until she's between the DJ booth and me. Tal would kill me for being here, for thwarting her years of effort to get me over this whole thing. She's always been appalled that none of them would speak to me after what happened, as if it were my fault. She thought that, by this point, *I* should be the one who isn't speaking to Elliot. But without seeing him again, I don't really get to make that choice, do I.

"You two dated?"

"No," I say. "Des's friend is the one I didn't date."

Louise is dancing up a storm; I struggle to keep cover. "I can't believe you conned me into coming to the outer boroughs to stalk a college boyfriend," she says.

"I just thought it was a sign," I say. "The last time I talked to any of them was that Halloween I turned twenty-one." It's hard, on the dance floor, over the music, to fill her in on what happened that night. *I* barely know. She pulls me closer to the wall, cranes her neck so her ear is right next to my lips as I tell her as best I can. "I read that Des was DJing a Halloween party and I thought maybe Elliot would be here, and we would run into each other and, I don't know, that something would have changed. Or, you know, that nothing would have."

"You did not think it was a sign," she says. "You don't be-lieve in signs."

Louise isn't Taline, but she does know me pretty well. "You're right," I tell her, scanning the room. There is no one else here I know. "We can go to Manhattan now if you want."

She throws her arms around me and guides me toward the door. "I'll get us a cab," she says.

DECISION MAKING FOR SAFE AND HEALTHY LIVING
Taline, 2006

I LET MYSELF INTO ZOE'S HOUSE, a two-bedroom ranch a few blocks from where we grew up as neighbors, and spot her sitting cross-legged on the floor, her two-year-old trying to wedge his head into her armpit while she balances her newborn in one arm and holds her cell phone in the other hand. I kick off my sandals and head right past the little family unit to the kitchen sink, where I scrub my hands up to my elbows. Then I drop down onto the nubby carpet and claim the baby, gathering her sweet sleeping self to my chest.

Growing up, Zoe and I were best friends, but now we're more like sisters. I don't mean to say that we are closer now than we used to be, although I also don't mean we're not.

Zoe winks at me, extracting herself from Billy's desperate grasp before running for the back porch, phone clenched to her ear. Billy stands up as if to follow her, but then seems to notice that I've got the baby in my arms. "*My* baby," he says. He points at her, a complicated motor skill that involves his thumb as much as his index finger. His blond hair is sticking out on one side, and his round tummy is exposed under his blue striped shirt. He looks enormous compared to the newborn.

"What's your baby's name?" I ask. "I haven't met her before." The baby is sleeping hard, her mouth open, a tiny, improbable snore escaping each time she exhales. She is entirely bald, dressed in a pink onesie with flaps folded over her hands so she won't scratch herself.

Billy screws up his face. "Minnie," he says, tentative. He looks around for his mother.

"I think it might be Maddie," I say. "Minnie is a mouse."

He contemplates this for a second, staring off to the side. Then, nodding, he says, "Maddie."

"You remember my name?" He is bashful, knowing he should know and yet he doesn't. I don't blame him, of course. I only make it out for a visit every few months, and in little-kid time, that's an eternity, like asking me to remember the name of someone I met ten years ago. "Taline," I say. Then, slower: "*Tal-een.*"

"*Tal-een* is coming for lunch," he says, repeating what Zoe must have been telling him all morning. He clenches his face again. "Taline?"

"Yes, Billy?"

"I have a poop," he says.

I sniff the air and can confirm. I lean back, trying to see what Zoe's doing out on the porch. She's pacing, and while she was mostly listening to the other person on the phone before, now she is the one talking. It doesn't look great, whatever is going on out there.

"I'm holding Maddie right now," I tell Billy. "I don't think I can do that and change your diaper."

He looks at me with both wispy eyebrows raised, like there's something major wrong with me.

"I wear underpants," he says.

"Good to know," I say, scooting so my back is up against the couch. The baby, all six-pounds-something of her, is getting heavy. I slide us around so that she is curled on my chest and hold her head steady with one hand. I'm not quite a pro at holding other people's babies, but I had some practice with Billy. I was surprised when Zoe told me she was pregnant again; I thought of her as such a new mom still. But Billy's not a baby; he's a person now, standing in front of me, rubbing his eyes with his fists and waiting to be entertained. With the hand not holding the baby, I point to his pile of books. "Pick one out," I say.

We make our way through quite the stack of animal stories before Zoe finally returns. "I am so sorry," she says.

"Don't apologize to me," I say. "Billy needs his diaper changed and thinks I'm incompetent for not being able to do it while holding the baby."

"You could have just put her in the bouncer," she says, gesturing. Then she pauses, adjusting the waistband of her stretch pants. "I mean, oh my God. First, of course you shouldn't have done that. Second—Billy doesn't wear diapers anymore." At this, he shoots me a triumphant look. "What are you supposed to do when you have to poo?" She hoists him up under her arm. "We'll be back in a few," she says. "Promise me you'll never have kids."

"I promise," I say. She pauses outside the bathroom door and looks at me over her shoulder.

"I'm kidding," she says. "So are you, right?"

*

We have lunch, a decadent spread of sushi I picked up in the city to celebrate Zoe being able to eat raw fish again—nine months without sushi was one of her main complaints about pregnancy—as well as a small chicken teriyaki for Billy, and then Zoe puts on a cartoon. Billy races around the couch three times, an expression of exuberant happiness, before settling down to watch. "Pre-Maddie, he got three episodes a week. I've upped his dosage," she says. She reaches behind her for a nursing cover, patterned with little sheep, and slides the baby under it, exposing a blue-veined boob as she does. "Sorry."

"You've got to stop apologizing," I tell her.

"Oh please," she says. "Me, me, me. What's going on with you?"

I pull my feet under me on her big cushy couch, the kind that wouldn't even fit through the door of my apartment. "Well, I'm working in an after-school program. In the interview, the director made it sound like I'd be teaching art, but really, it's mostly homework help. I think it's good experience, but the hours are awful, and the pay is worse." Zoe nods along, her bloodshot eyes trained on me, telegraphing that she's listening so hard, I think she can't possibly be.

"Alex?" she asks.

When Alex graduated our MFA program and headed back to New York, and I came with him even though I still had a year to go, no one was very happy with me. Not my advisor, even though it didn't seem like she thought I had much potential. Not my parents, who assumed—rightly—that dropping out limited my job prospects. Not Val, who had just moved to Austin. Who I'd convinced to apply there. Who was supposed to share my apartment. No, no one was happy with me except for Zoe, who thought it was all very romantic.

"He's all right," I say. And he is, I'm sure. He's the kind of guy who's always doing just fine. I don't feel like going into it, how we broke up almost as soon as we moved back here and he has work in two group shows as we speak, while all I have is an easel wedged into the corner of a bedroom, the bedroom itself wedged into the corner of a loft I'm sharing with three other people I barely know. Zoe wouldn't get it. Zoe's got enough to think about right now. She opens her mouth like she might ask a rare follow-up question, so I veer left. "Are you going to tell me about that phone call or what?"

"I was hoping it would be over by the time you got here," she says, switching the baby to the other side.

"Does that hurt?" I ask.

She nods toward Billy. "That one hurt," she says. "With this one, I don't feel much. He might have killed my nerve endings before she got to them. I'm pretty over it, though. I sent Brian to the store for formula yesterday, but he came back claiming he couldn't figure out which one to buy."

"Wait," I say, "we digressed. The phone call."

"Don't get mad," she says.

"Mad?" I repeat. I haven't been mad at her since fifth grade, when she told me that she was getting her ears pierced even though I wasn't allowed yet. If I got mad at her every time I probably should have, we'd never have made it this far.

"That's not the right word. Just, don't think this is bad." She looks at me with her mouth pursed. "Remember Officer Bradley?"

"Our D.A.R.E. officer?" I ask. I can picture him in his uniform, buttoned too tight across his broad chest, his hair spiked, standing with meaty legs spread in front of our middle school health class, warning us about the irrevocable dangers of smoking one marijuana cigarette.

"I'm not having an affair, if that's what you're thinking." Zoe pulls at the waistband of her stretch pants again. She props the baby on her shoulder, palming her back to burp her, and clicks the remote to put on another show—or is it just the same one again?—for Billy. "He pulled me over a few months ago. Billy was with Brian at a Mets game. Side note—he slept through the whole thing and Brian was appalled. I wasn't speeding, I was—actually, I was on the phone with you. Remember?"

I do remember. She was midsentence when the sirens started but called back later that night as if nothing had happened.

"So, he was about to write me a ticket and then he straight up recognized me. I was embarrassed—we were such dorks in middle school." I frown at being implicated. "But, like, he gave those stupid anti-drug speeches to bazillions of kids, and he remembered me? We all used to think he was so hot. I mean, it's a little flattering, right?"

I shrug. Sure.

"He lets me go, I thank him, and I continue to Dressler's to have a burger, kid-free. I was already pregnant, although not really showing, and you remember I had that serious red meat phase? Ten minutes later, he shows up there, too. His shift had ended and he wanted a beer. I invite him to sit with me. We talk and talk, and then, after that, we wind up texting. A few hours on the phone every now and then. He asked me to drinks a few times, but I always had a good excuse."

I squint, watch her run her finger up and down the soft fuzz on the back of her baby's head. Zoe was the first friend I knew to get married. She'd called shrieking that he'd "finally" proposed to her down the shore, at sunset: a Jersey girl dream. I still felt very young, but Zoe and Brian seemed ready to get on with it: the jobs, the house, the kids. And—they seemed happy. Am I naive to think anyone's relationship is beyond reproach? Zoe is talking to me about a police officer of our youth.

I get two glasses of water from the kitchen, pass her one, and take a long sip of mine. "Do you think," I say, slowly, "that he could have run your plate and found out your name before coming to your window?"

Zoe bites through her thumbnail; I cringe at the muffled crack. "Hmph."

"What's the rest of the story?" I ask. "Get to the phone call."

"Well, he pulled me over again," she says. "Like, just before Maddie was born. He came to the window with this big grin, and then—God, Tali, you should have seen how his face fell. Billy was in the car; my belly was ludicrous. It occurred to me I hadn't been wearing my wedding ring at Dressler's because my fingers were already so swollen."

"Nothing happened, though," I say. "Like, physically. Even emotionally, for you, really."

She shakes her head hard, her hair flying. "You know how you just felt reading that stack of books with Billy? Imagine that's your everyday—literally, your entire every day. Not that babies aren't a blessing. Babies *are* a blessing. I love every minute. But I was bored, honestly, and figured Colin was texting a million other equally bored housewives. If what he says is to be believed, though, he had this whole fantasy based around me. He thought we were taking it slow."

"Why the call today?" I ask. "If he pulled you over a few weeks ago already?"

"I haven't picked up," she says. "He called from a different number today. He's been driving by the house. Yesterday, I think I saw him parked around the corner."

"Not to be alarmist," I say, "but he has a gun, you know? Should you tell Brian?"

She widens her eyes. "I should *not*."

Billy stands up, turns, and says, "Mama, poop."

Without missing a beat, she passes the baby to me, grabs Billy, and bounds toward the bathroom. I stare into Maddie's sleepy, wrinkled face, the lines, bumps, and blotches that have not yet smoothed out and plumped up into baby perfection. I fold back the little flaps on her onesie; her fingernails are the smallest things I've ever seen. I hold her close; she roots around like she wants to nurse. I can't even imagine what that would feel like. It's like trying to imagine a sixth sense.

I stand up, bouncing her and pacing, until I stop to study a framed picture collage of Zoe and Brian's wedding. She was only twenty-two and looks unbearably beautiful in her gigantic poofy princess gown. There were ten of us bridesmaids, all wearing matching strapless satin dresses. Zoe hired someone to do hair and makeup for all of us. I tried to resist, to explain that I'd rather do my own, but she wouldn't let me get away with it. She knew that, left to my own devices, I would have my hair in my face, black eyeliner, and not much else. All done up in the photos, I am practically unrecognizable, my hair curled and stuck with a giant rose, my lips lined and painted the same sort of brown as all the other girls. I look like I'm in Jersey drag.

Billy tears out of the bathroom, pants-less.

"What do you feed this kid that he poops so much?" I ask.

She shakes her head. "He says it sometimes to get attention from me—it's like the one thing he does I can't ignore. He didn't have to go, and he won't put his pants back on." She shrugs. "Who cares, right?"

"Exactly," I say. "No pants, no problem." We both admire Billy's round bum, then laugh as he yawns and rubs his eyes. Zoe catches his yawn. I look at the clock. It's a delicate thing, visiting a friend with a new baby. "I should go," I say.

Zoe nods. "I think it's naptime here."

I kiss Billy's head. Staring open-mouthed, he refuses to say goodbye. Zoe rolls her eyes, hugs me, and takes back Maddie. The baby stretches, extending one arm and bending the other like she's about to fly off to fight crime, a reflex Zoe told me about when Billy was a newborn. "Bye, Superwoman," I say to her. I whisper in Zoe's ear, "Don't answer the phone again. All unknown calls to go voicemail."

She gives me a salute, but then says, "Yeah, okay."

By the front door, I pick my well-worn shoes off the rack that also holds Billy's tiny blue Velcro sneakers, Brian's Adidas slides, and what looks like thirty-five pairs of Zoe's flip-flops, in every color and shade imaginable. Then I head out, easing the door shut behind me.

Zoe's lawn is so perfectly manicured, her car shiny, black, and enormous. It has one of those stick-figure-drawing stickers on the rear window: Brian, Zoe, and Billy waving at me. They need to update it now that Maddie's here. I wonder what Zoe and I would have made of ourselves now, back when we were kids. Or I don't. Looking at the outlines of our lives, we both have at least some of what we'd wanted back then. I don't think we'd realize what we're missing.

The walk to my mom's house takes about ten minutes, just slightly longer than it did when Zoe lived in her childhood home a few blocks from here. I jag across the lawn, taking a shortcut through a few backyards. As I do, I see, just up the block, a cop car. Lights off, not idling, just parked there on the street. Is he inside? I crane my head, trying to see. There's definitely someone inside. As I head up the street, I can't help wondering what the hell Zoe was thinking. What did she expect, texting with a cop? Although, back then, we did think he was hot, back when we were taught that cops were here to help. Zoe might still believe that. The boys our age and teen idols we'd loved were so skinny; it had been a shocking thing to see the contours of Officer Bradley's body in his uniform. Did he wear it that tight on purpose? I almost wish that Zoe had slept with him so she could tell me what it was like. But I believe her that she didn't. If she says it's over, it's over. The nerve of this guy, bothering a woman with a newborn.

I pause on the sidewalk, pluck a shiny dark-green leaf from a hedge, and crumple it in my hand. I'm a good friend, right? The last thing Zoe needs is this dude hovering around her. I turn around. I'm tentative, approaching the car. I half think it isn't him, that I'll get close and it won't be. Even when I'm right up next to the window, because of the way the sun bounces off of it, I can't tell. I see myself, not who's inside. I'm pale. I bite my lips to make them redder. My heart!—I can hear my blood in my ears. The instant before I raise my fist to rap on the glass, I know I shouldn't do it, but it's too late. The window is already lowering. My own reflection scrolls past and disappears. I look at him through the open window, a breeze moving through my hair. His eyes are the bright blue of his uniform. He says, "Taline?"

CLEAR BLUE
Tova, 2007

TOVA LIFTS HER LINEN SKIRT, squatting over the toilet, and positions the plastic cup in what she hopes is the right place. Three months of this and she still can't quite aim right. She collects enough pee to do the trick, washes her hands, and peels open the envelope containing the little paper stick. She dips it in the half-centimeter she's supposed to, counts—one Mississippi, two Mississippi, three Mississippi—then lays it flat before setting a timer for three minutes.

She tries to spend these moments of pause productively, but today she stares out her kitchen window. It is the first day of the fall semester and the first day in more than twenty-five years that Tova doesn't have a class to attend. The sections of lit theory she teaches start up later this week, but that's not the same as being a student herself. A woman with short hair, a giant purple backpack, and practical sandals hustles by, the Platonic ideal of a grad student. Tova envies her. Tova knows how to be good at school. Excellent, in fact. How are three minutes not up already? She washes a ceramic dish from breakfast and dries it with a special Scandinavian towel that is supposed to be extra-absorbent but seems, if anything, less so. Finally, the timer trills.

And there it is: two lines. She's ovulating. These damn predictors seem foolproof, and she can't understand why no one told her about them before a friend gave her half an open box this summer. For fifteen months she had been charting her erratic temperature to no avail and timing sex to coincide with certain days of the month—days that she now knows were totally arbitrary. Rather than on a schedule, her ovaries release eggs whenever they feel like it. Years of birth control—which she'd started taking in high school for her skin—masked the fact that an entire system in her body had gone rogue. Her gynecologist said, "I spend the first ten years I see patients helping them *not to* get pregnant and the next ten years helping them *to* get pregnant."

Later, lying on a blanket in the park with her friend Jasmine, Tova recounts this comment. "She said ten years?" Jasmine asks.

"That's what I thought, too," Tova says. "Not particularly encouraging. Thank goodness we're young. You know, youngish." She pops a little yellow tomato into her mouth and rolls it over her tongue. She's been in Northern California for half a decade and the produce is still a revelation. "Somehow, I had no idea that you only get two days a month when it can really happen, and you can't have sex both of those days because then the sperm won't mature. Like, what? But the advice I hear the most is to have fun. Don't get stressed out. *Have fun?*"

Jasmine rolls over on her side to wink at Tova. "I mean, sex with Elliot always has to be a little fun, right?" This thing with

Elliot still surprises Tova. With his outsize nose and skinny, bowed legs, he's not traditionally attractive and has never been smooth or charming in any kind of obvious way. Jasmine, a friend from college who lives out here now, too, isn't the only one of her classmates who seems to have had a crush on him back then, though. Sure, Tova likes him, but his cult sex symbol status was lost on her in college, when he was just her weird, sullen friend.

"I'm probably the problem on the fun front," Tova says. Jasmine doesn't react to this; Tova imagines she's thinking, Right.

"Anyway," Jasmine says, "tonight's the night?"

"Except." Tova starts laughing. She laughs so hard a tiny tomato seed flies out of her nose. "Elliot is at a monastery."

Jasmine sits up. "Say what?"

Tova sits up, too, crossing her legs and tucking her now wrinkled skirt between them. "It's a departmental retreat. He claims to think it's silly, but secretly he likes it. They're kicking off the semester with some intense, I don't know, whatever philosophers do. Intense philosophizing. He's there two more days. I can't begrudge him—we didn't know when it would happen this month. It's just that now we have to wait another month to try. Or three weeks. Or six."

"Call him," Jasmine says. "Or drive out there."

"Apparently, they don't have cell service—I guess that's part of the point. And he's got the car."

Jasmine sighs. "Okay, okay," she says. "I'll drive you."

*

They head out of town in Jasmine's pristine vintage car. As they drive, Jasmine says, "I almost asked if you put on nice underwear, but then I thought, I bet Tova only has nice underwear."

"Thanks?" Tova twists her hair over her shoulder.

"Confirm or deny," Jasmine says, snapping her minty gum. "I actually want to know."

"Confirm," Tova says. "It's all lace, and I hand-wash it, and it gets replaced at the first sign of wear. But, what? I can hardly see you in old, stretched-out granny panties."

Jasmine has black hair cut into curved pinup bangs, winged eyeliner, and a little indent in her cheek that is actually a piercing, not a dimple. "I have the full spectrum," she says. "The nice stuff comes out when someone else is going to see it. So it all stays in the drawer now, more or less. The briefs I'm wearing I've had since I was, like, eighteen."

"Why's it all in the drawer?" The drive is beautiful now that they're chugging toward nature. There are pink flowers tangled in the roadside shrubbery and the late-afternoon sun is still bright. They're listening to Dolly Parton and she's belting out her song about a new day dawning, but she could be singing about the way the sky looks right now. Tova cracks the window to let in the incredible green smell of the outdoors.

"I've decided to be celibate."

Jasmine's eyes are trained on the road, so Tova can't tell if she's being serious. She's always admired the way Jasmine treats hooking up: like recreation, sport. Tova says, "And I'm making you drive me to a monastery so I can have sex?"

"It's cool—I'm happy for other people to get busy. I'm

thinking I'll do it—or not do it—for a year. It'll do me good to concentrate on work, and friends, and, like, yoga."

"Imagine giving our twenty-year-old selves a glimpse of this conversation," Tova says.

"Seriously, when all we wanted to do was fuck!" Jasmine cracks up.

"You know," Tova says, pausing and wondering if she really wants to say what she's about to say. How much more intimate does she want this whole thing to get? "I actually didn't sleep with anyone in college. No one at all."

For this, Jasmine takes her eyes off the road. "I don't believe you for a second," she says. "You were so tiny and beautiful and that party house you lived in? Men were in and out of there every day. You didn't even sleep with Elliot?"

"I should have," Tova says. "Not with Elliot, but with other people. Especially if I knew we'd wind up together and that would be the end of it. He's the only person I've ever slept with! It's not like I was religious or saving myself or waiting for love or something. I just wouldn't do it."

Jasmine takes her hand off the wheel to point a manicured nail at Tova as she diagnoses. "You liked saying no."

Tova thinks back on her younger self. She used to kiss people like it didn't matter. Indiscriminately, almost. It was a way to disarm them—different from Jasmine's carefree approach, but two sides of the same coin, really—a way to exert power. "You're right," she says. "I liked saying no."

"Meanwhile, I . . ."

Tova laughs. "Didn't you keep a notebook with a tally in it? Like some sort of deranged frat boy?"

"You know it," she says. "Color-coded and everything. I still can't decide if I was being subversive or, like, a twisted servant of the patriarchy."

"We should have split the difference," Tova says.

"No way," Jasmine says. "I earned all those tally marks."

*

The monastery is painted American cheese yellow, with terra-cotta tiles on the roof and bright red impatiens spilling out of hanging planters all along the façade. Its cheery colors are slightly dampened by the eerie cast of twilight. "I'm going to drop you off and drive to town for a coffee," Jasmine says.

"This is really awkward," Tova says. "I can't believe you did this for me."

Jasmine leans across Tova and opens her door. "Just name the baby after me, okay?"

*

Tova worries there will be a gauntlet to get through on her way into the building—security, receptionists, lots of explaining to do—but the iron-embellished door swings open when she pushes it. Before setting off for the monastery, she'd changed into a gauzy white dress with a skirt that flares out when she moves. Elliot likes this dress because of all the little buttons down the front, which she lets him undo even though they're a hassle to refasten.

Inside, standing in the dim foyer, she pauses to let her eyes adjust and listens. It's unnerving, the way the arches and tiles reflect sound. As voices double and redouble on themselves, she could be hearing chatting or chanting, trapped birds or the ghosts of monks past. One of the first lessons she'll teach this semester is on defamiliarization. Her students will look for and find it everywhere on the page, but she feels it here, in the body. Or, disembodied—her husband divorced from space and time, his presence in the ether. Everything concrete she knows about ceilings and floors, Elliot's solidity, the exact contours of his face, seems, now, uncertain. Elliot once asked her if studying literature through the lens of theory took the magic out of it. "It helps you name the magic," she'd said. "And puts some of it into your hands." She is in the building, and so is Elliot, and she can find him.

She heads left. Turning a corner, she is on a balcony rimming a courtyard of sorts, although it is indoors. She smells marijuana and, what, pizza? The philosophers are below, lounging, eating, and gossiping. Their voices were coming from both everywhere and nowhere because they were essentially below her. She peers down at them from behind a stucco column and recognizes everyone except for a few, probably the newest recruits. The department chair is sitting cross-legged on the floor, gesticulating with a joint burning down between his fingers, his gray hair alive with head-shaking opinion. Elliot takes up an entire couch, lying on his back, his legs extended up onto the arm and his long hair tangled under his head. Tova wonders what he's thinking, relaxing like that while the seventy-something-year-old professor is down on the ground.

One benefit to him hogging the couch, though, is that he is the only one with his eyes uplifted. Tova nudges the leaves on a tall potted rubber plant on the balcony beside her, hoping the slight movement will attract his attention. When that doesn't work, she attempts telepathy. *Elliot, Elliot, look up.* She sidesteps the plant, placing herself in indirect view of the group downstairs, a sliver of her edging out into the open, and raises her hand. This works—too well. There's one scream—a woman Tova doesn't know pointing and shrieking—then another. Tova covers her mortified expression with her arm and waves. She hears Elliot say, "That's not a ghost. That's my wife."

*

He finds her crouching by the rubber plant. His shoulders are tense and his eyes wild. Of course he'd think the worst with her showing up like this. There was this movie they watched once, an indie it seems maybe no one else saw, about a group of friends who go to a yoga retreat in the country, and then a nuclear winter destroys the rest of the world. "Everything is fine," she says, leaping to her feet and hugging him. "I'm sorry I freaked everyone out."

The worry evaporates from his face as he steps back and studies hers. "It's cool," he says. But he's still waiting for her to explain herself.

She hooks her fingers into the hem of his soft black T-shirt. Should she just explain, or try to make this seem, what, sexy? Because they had been friends for so long, they really do eschew all that. Not that they don't have sex; they do. But she's either sexy to him or she's not—she doesn't try, not usually. The lace underwear has nothing to do with him. She draws close to his ear. "It's time," she whispers.

He scratches the back of his neck and Tova tries not to be mad at him for being high. He doesn't remember that they have a goal in mind. She wants to finish her dissertation while she's pregnant and for the baby to be a year old before she starts a tenure-track job. Yes, they're young, but she still feels like their time is running short. To hammer out all those plans with someone who can be as quiet and interior as Elliot—they are hard-won, and she doesn't want to abandon them. She gestures in the vague direction of her uterus, when what she wants is to knee him in the groin. "I took a test, and it said *now*."

"Oh!" he says, too loudly. Tova hears a rustle downstairs; they must all be wondering what the hell is going on. Elliot's face opens with understanding; he looks vulnerable and sweet as he smiles. The crease where he has a scar on his jaw catches the light. He grabs her hand, and they feel their way down a long, unlit hallway.

He pulls her into a room with two narrow beds in it. The door doesn't lock, which probably doesn't matter, but he uses his hip to shove a small desk in front of it anyway. The rest of the space is almost entirely bare except for his backpack on the floor, spilling black T-shirts, and his roommate's neater, still-packed rolling suitcase up against the wall. The room's one adornment is a thin wooden cross hanging between the beds. He tries to undo the stupid buttons on her dress but only makes it past the top two. "Just lift it up," she says.

She leans back on the cot as he pushes her dress to her navel. "Missionary in the monastery," he says.

He's turned on. Why wouldn't he be? He's not doing anything wrong, she tells herself, trying to figure out why she wants to cry. She wants to think, to feel, that this is hot, too. But there's this question: What if it doesn't work? What if it never does?

After, as she holds still with her knees drawn to her chest, Tova asks, "What are you going to tell everyone?"

"You don't want me to tell the truth?" he teases, weaving his fingers in between hers. He's sitting on the edge of the bed; it's too narrow for the two of them to lie side by side.

"I'd prefer not," she says. Her hips hurt. She always thinks, Maybe it would have happened if I just kept my legs elevated a few more minutes.

"I'll say I forgot my inhaler," he says. Elliot's had asthma ever since he was jumped in college. That's the conclusion Tova came to, anyway—he never seemed to have trouble breathing before the punctured lung. "That you saw it on the counter and rushed up here, just in case. Which—wait, how *did* you get here?"

"Jasmine drove me," Tova says. "*Jasmine.* I should go."

*

Outside, it is completely dark. Tova expects the giant car to be there waiting for her, headlights illuminating a path from the monastery, but maybe Jasmine assumed that this would take even longer than it did? They were quick, once it got down to it. Tova sends a text: *ready when you are.*

She sits on a step to wait with her legs pulled to her chest, in a slight recline. Will it help? The opposite advice would be ludicrous: To make sure you don't get pregnant, stand up right away. Stretch. Shake your hips around. Imagine telling that to a teenager.

Tova fixes the buttons on her white dress. She wishes she'd worn another color. When she was little, she used to love hearing the story of how she was born in a snowstorm, her parents battling through snowdrifts and whiteouts to get to the hospital just in time. In tribute, she dressed as a blizzard every year for Halloween: at two, at twelve, at twenty. She'd wear white dresses and boots, white nail polish, sometimes white wigs or white turbans, and always lots of snowy sparkles. She gave up that costume when Elliot was attacked, though, because it became associated with what happened. Just like Jell-O shots, that girl Val who caused the whole thing, spin the bottle, even eggs. She flinches every time she cracks one. That Halloween, Jasmine wore nothing but a flag—French? Italian?—a thong, and a wig, cut in much the same way her actual hair is now. Before it all went down, Tova remembers she could see Elliot and Jasmine's tongues when they kissed during spin the bottle. They went at it with more gusto than she thought appropriate for the game, but it was still a few years before she could even identify why this bothered her, when she usually so respected Jasmine's frank sexuality.

Maybe she hadn't been put off before by the white dress because it's a sundress. She should donate it.

Tova considers going back inside—she hasn't used the bathroom since leaving home three hours ago—but doesn't want to disrupt the philosophers again. She sends Jasmine another text and taps her toes. She takes some notes for teaching although she's already planned out what she's going to teach almost to the minute, and besides, she's taught these same courses before. Finally, after almost an hour, Jasmine's car screams through the darkness and stops short in front of her.

Tova climbs in and Jasmine steps on the gas, gunning it around the circular driveway, even though they can barely see where the pavement stops and the landscaping begins.

"I'm sorry I didn't see your texts until a few minutes ago," Jasmine says, turning to Tova for a second, perfectly arched eyebrows raised. "Cell service is terrible here. But so? Was Elliot happy to see you?"

Cell service—of course. "They all thought I was a ghost at first," Tova says. "Then he thought I was there to deliver terrible news. So yeah, when he found out why I was really there, he was happy."

"You downplay how much he loves you," Jasmine says, taking her eyes off the road for too long to give Tova an accusing look. "I see how he looks at you. The idea of Elliot Thomas *ever* looking at someone the way he looks at you!"

Tova doesn't deny that Elliot loves her, but it's nothing like the way Jasmine perceives it. It would be nice if it were true, but it just isn't. "Honestly, Jasmine," she says, "sometimes I think Elliot and I should have just stayed friends."

"I don't get you," Jasmine says. Does she sound angry?

The road leading from the monastery is narrow and full of twists; Tova notices it now more than on the way there. Jasmine is flying around the curves. She's accelerating when she should be taking it slow. Tova grips her seat as the car goes faster and faster.

"I need you to pull over," Tova says. "I'm going to throw up." It is the only thing she can think to say.

"Oh, sweetie!" Jasmine says. Tova doesn't hear any actual concern in Jasmine's voice, but she does turn the wheel and veer off the road.

She doesn't slow down enough, though. They skid. There's a thud, and an ominous hiss. It's not a crash, per se—they aren't jolted very hard, and it isn't clear that they've hit something. There's no tree or wall in front of them. When Jasmine screams, it is belated. They're fine.

Tova takes a cautious step out of the car. She breathes in a few lungfuls of the cool, piney night air to calm herself before she looks down. They've driven onto a pile of construction debris. It shouldn't have been there, but Jasmine should have pulled over more carefully. The front passenger tire is blown out. Tova leans into the car. "Flat tire," she says.

Jasmine is still in her seat, belt buckled, as if she expects they'll be on their way again in a moment. "Can we drive on it?"

"No," Tova says. She needs to pee so badly that her stomach hurts from clenching. She wipes a bit of sweat from her forehead and tries not to be mad; what will that help?

Jasmine bites her lower lip. "I don't have a spare."

"Triple A?" Tova climbs back into her seat.

Jasmine shakes her head.

Tova says, "You know what, I have it."

It takes Tova a few moments to fish the card out of her wallet, call, and explain the situation to the dispatcher. When she hangs up, she says, "The good news is that the nausea passed. The bad is that the tow truck will be a while. And I have to pee."

"There are tissues in the glove compartment," Jasmine says, nodding toward the trees just past the debris.

Tova wonders if she can hold it. This is another one—non-sensical, unscientific. She always worries that she's disrupting the process when she uses the bathroom too soon after sex. Even though she knows that's not how it works. That's not how it works, she tells herself again. She grabs a few tissues and picks her way around the rebar to find a spot behind a tree.

Back in the car, a certain sour smell comes into focus. She'd noticed it before, right when Jasmine picked her up at the monastery, but it hadn't clicked. She wrinkles her nose, considering. "You didn't go get a coffee, did you."

"That's not why this happened, though," Jasmine says, quickly, like she'd been expecting Tova to mention something. "It was impossible to see all that junk by the side of the road."

"Yeah, but . . ." Tova says. They still have hours to spend together, but she can't keep the sharpness out of her voice.

"I didn't have that much," Jasmine says.

Jasmine has always been a big drinker, but Tova assumed when she was talking about the celibacy, the yoga, and the focus on work, she also meant to undertake a change in this regard, too. "I think you did, actually," Tova says.

"I always knew that's how you felt," Jasmine says.

"Always as in since I smelled the wine on your breath thirty seconds ago?" Tova keeps a futile watch in the side-view mirror, hoping they'll be rescued sooner rather than later.

"You know what I mean," Jasmine says. "Everything is 'who me?' with you, you know? You are perfect in every way and have the guy everyone else wanted, but who you don't seem to really want yourself, and you act like you don't even know what the big deal is. Like it just all comes naturally to you, when the rest of us have to really *strive*."

Is this what other people think of her, too? Even if some

of what Jasmine is saying is true, it's not up to her to say it. The inappropriateness doesn't mitigate the sting, though. Tova leans her head back and traces her eyes around an improbable coffee stain on the ceiling.

"I'd say this whole errand disproves your theory, no?" she asks. "My own body is in revolt against what I want most. And I don't know what any of this has to do with you drinking too much."

Jasmine exhales. Her breath is so acrid Tova isn't sure how she missed it before.

"We better change seats," Tova says.

"It's not like the tow truck driver would call the police," Jasmine says, unbuckling her seat belt and coming around anyway. They've barely finished settling into their seats when Tova sees Jasmine wiping her eyes. "I was just thinking," she says. "You could be pregnant, and I got you into a car crash because I was feeling sorry for myself."

"It's fine," Tova says. "We are fine."

"Really?" Jasmine asks.

If Tova answered honestly, she would say no. But that's when she notices Jasmine isn't looking at her. At least, not at her face. Tova follows her friend's gaze downward, to the hands resting in her lap. Except that isn't what they're doing. She's holding them, fingers woven together, around her middle. Jasmine is reading her gesture one way, but Tova knows she's wrong.

What she's doing now, Tova understands, is what she's been doing this whole time. Her hands aren't folded over her stomach in protection—or not only that. They are clasped there: an act of prayer.

LANDMARK DECISIONS
Valerie, 2007

I PUKE THE WHOLE PLANE RIDE TO PITTSBURGH, a lethal combination of morning and motion sickness. Dramamine—like whiskey, runny eggs, and smoked fish—is off-limits to the pregnant, at least per my particular doctor. As Marc secures the rental car—a toaster-shaped Nissan—and we load in for the drive to his grandmother's senior living facility, I'm crunching on ice from the airport coffee shop, trying to rehydrate. The cubes squeak between my teeth. Marc suggests I dip some napkins in the cold water at the bottom of the cup and apply compresses to my eyes for the ride.

"They're that puffy?" I ask.

"Just a little," he says. He reaches over to squeeze my knee. "Thanks for doing this with me."

"Hands on the wheel, please," I say, although Marc is a driver at home in any situation. He's maneuvering with no problem. I'm the one who takes weeks to adapt.

"Sorry, sweetie," he says, adjusting his grip at ten and two.

For the past two months, Marc has been truly solicitous,

fetching green grapes when that was all I could eat, then plain bagels when carbs became the only thing that didn't sit funny in my gut. The other day, during my eight-week obstetrician appointment, he clutched my hand between both of his as the impossible heartbeat flickered on the technician's screen, tears gathering at the corners of his eyes. So much of pregnancy is a mystery, but there is no mystery to Marc. There was his love, his excitement, and his fear. Right on his face.

It never would have crossed my mind to invite him to the appointment. But after Taline got over the shock of discovering she was the first person to hear about that little plus sign materializing on the pregnancy test, she said, "He better be the first one to see the heartbeat, then."

"I don't know what to think about things unless we talk them out first," I told her.

"If you're having a baby with him, he's got to start being the first one you go to," she said. So I brought him to the exam, and she was right about that, but I still don't know if she's right about the other piece of it. Does your partner always have to be the one dearest to you?

We've been instructed to let Grandma Dinah know when we're leaving the airport. Marc tried when we landed and again when we loaded up the car; the phone was busy each time. I redial every five minutes as we merge from one unfamiliar road to the next, finally pulling into the parking lot of the Gershwin Senior Living Apartments. We find Dinah's spot, number seventeen; she still pays for it even though Marc's father convinced her to give up her car. It wasn't long after Dinah relinquished her Lincoln that she had her fall. Now she's using a wheelchair and relocating from the second floor of Gershwin to a more accessible apartment on the first. We're here to help her with the move, although why all the housing in a place like this isn't accessible is beyond me.

As Marc exits the car, I flip down the mirror. My cheeks are gaunt from the weeks of vomiting, there is a fine network of busted capillaries around my eyes, and my hair is stringy with sweat at the temples. At that eight-week ultrasound, as the technician squirted gel on her wand and had me scoot to the end of the exam table, she assured me that my symptoms would pass "really soon." She wasn't a doctor, but she did have a certain level of expertise, so I believed her. It was the promise of relief I felt then that made seeing the pulsing spot of the interloper inside of me, that blip on her screen, all the more shocking. We hadn't been trying to get pregnant, and I wasn't prepared for the prospect of sharing the real estate of my body. I recoiled in the way I do when I feel an uninvited hand glance across my breast in the subway. Thinking I was cold, Marc helped me by pulling the industrial green sheet, soft from being washed so many times, to cover my knees.

There'd been so much to do with moving back to New York, setting up our apartment together, and starting a new job; I kept looking down at my pack of birth control pills and realizing that I was off—I'd forgotten one at some point, or was it two, three? It was on my to-do list to switch methods to something with less room for error. But then this happened. We wanted kids, Marc and I, eventually. He was so happy when I told him that for a second, looking at his lit-up face, I thought—wait, am I happy, too? So I'm working on coming around, but the havoc the pregnancy is wreaking on my body doesn't make it easy.

Climbing out of the car, the air feels cool and still. "This is the part of the country least prone to natural disasters," Marc says. "There are vaults in the mountains filled with film archives and precious artwork. It's the safest possible place to be."

We've only just moved back to New York, but now Marc seems ready to buy a house in the suburbs to "raise our family." I've let it slide when he's brought up New Jersey, which is barely a half hour from where we live, but now that he seems to be hinting at a move farther afield I can't help but roll my eyes.

I flash to these alternate timelines sometimes: The one where I leaned in to kiss Elliot instead of waiting for him to kiss me. The one where Taline didn't go to Austin, or where I didn't follow her. Louise practically runs FreeLove now; what if I'd stayed there? The timeline where I didn't go to that one house party and write my number on Marc's hand. I never thought I'd get married and pregnant before I turned thirty. I know plenty of people do—it is utterly normal. But that's not the idea I had of myself. I can't help but feel like Taline's choices have brought me here more than my own. When I saw that plus sign on the pregnancy test, I called to hear her reassuring voice in my ear, but also to blame her. What would happen to me if I left the city again?

"New York is the country's safest big city," I say, following Marc as he weaves through the parked cars toward the senior center, rolling both of our carry-on suitcases behind him. "And if I'm having a baby, I'm having a New Yorker."

"If," he says.

I don't know what is wrong with me, always being the one to make his face fall. "When," I correct. We stop right outside the door and as it opens for us, I am hit with a wall of warmth and an overwhelming odor. I gag a little, even though it isn't objectively unpleasant. "What's that smell?"

"Sugar," Marc says, sniffing. "And cinnamon. Blintzes, maybe. Or kugel. Apparently, the cafeteria here is pretty good."

Kugel, I think. I could maybe stomach that.

*

The attendant at the building's entrance welcomes us in—"She's been talking about your visit for weeks!"—and guides us to a first-floor apartment, already equipped with welcome mat, mezuzah, and decorative wreath. Dinah flings open the door a moment later, four foot ten and scowling. "You said you'd call first!" she says, impeccably penciled eyebrows raised. "I'm still a mess."

"The phone was busy!" Marc bends to kiss her on the cheek. "You look great."

"Psh," she scoffs, gesturing at the cloud of gray-blue hair frosting her head. She bats him away, grabs me by the wrist, and pulls me inside. "Valerie! Skinny, skinny," she says, smacking me on the rear. We follow her into an apartment that appears as if it's been lived in for decades. There are islands of plush area rugs spreading across the already carpeted floor, elaborate treatments above the windows, and sideboards heavily populated by bric-a-brac. Canisters of flour, tins of tea, and Tupperware containers of cookies are stacked on the galley kitchen's counters. Not a moving box in sight.

"Did we get it backwards?" I whisper to Marc. "Is she moving upstairs?"

"Grandma, is this your new apartment already?" Marc asks.

"Oh, yes," she responds. "It's wonderful." When he issues a follow-up question—but how?—she shoots me a conspiratorial look, poking her thumb at him. "We have luxuries like movers in Pennsylvania, too, you know. How was your flight?"

"Quick," Marc says.

"Easy trip," Dinah says, ferrying a cut-glass platter piled with cookies to the coffee table in the living room. "You could visit more."

Marc winks at me. "I'm sure we will," he says. "It was harder when we were in school."

"Texas," she grunts, sliding into a large wicker chair, a flea market throne. She gestures to the blue-and-white couch across from her and we take a seat. "That I never understood. Cowboys, big hair, and the Shrub."

"The Shrub?" I ask.

"That's her name for Bush," Marc says.

Dinah nods. "But Obama," she says. "The speeches he gives—that's what I call presidential. Your grandfather would have had other thoughts, but . . . have a mandelbrot."

Marc and I reach for our cookies. I take a tiny mouse-bite, letting the dry crumbs dissolve on my tongue. Before any of it even reaches my stomach, I feel my system mounting a protest, but what can I do—not take Grandma's cookies?

Something hard is poking me from between the couch cushions. I reach down and pull out a cordless phone, beeping off the hook now that it isn't muffled by the pillows. "Here's why your phone was busy," I say, looking for the cradle on the end table.

Dinah shakes her head. "No," she says. "I've been here all along."

*

Feeling leaden, I beg a nap and Dinah directs us to her bedroom. The floral chintz comforter crackles with static each time I move. I say, "I can't believe she is planning to sleep on the couch tonight."

"You heard her," Marc says. He's dozing next to me, although he has never been good at naps. "The conviction! I truly don't know how we could have gotten her to change her mind."

"Honestly, this bed is so uncomfortable that maybe she prefers the couch." Even if Marc and I wanted to be closer to each other, the tented shape of the mattress would make it impossible. We move to the middle but slide to our respective outer edges before long.

"Should I tell her we're already pregnant?" he asks. "That if her plan was to keep us apart on this thing, it failed miserably?"

At first, Marc didn't understand why we couldn't tell people right away—he wanted to call our parents, our friends, throw a parade. He thought I was being unnecessarily pessimistic when I explained that everyone we told, we would have to un-tell if something happened. My friend Isabel was at sixteen weeks when her doctor couldn't find what had been, initially, a robust heartbeat. When I reminded Marc about her miscarriage, he said he hadn't known—he said it was news to him. Well, what do you think happened when she didn't wind up with a baby?

I asked. He shrugged. At least he looked embarrassed at never having wondered.

Part of me would be relieved if it happened that way for us—just a quiet disappearance. Of course, I have the text messages documenting what Isabel went through: anything but quiet, anything but forgotten.

After Marc proposed just eighteen months after we met, and I, in shock, accepted, Taline said to me, "Marriage is just you saying, 'I choose this person now.' You can un-choose him at any time, right? We've got this great thing called divorce." Pregnancy, so far, is full body nausea and the realization that, if there's a baby, there can be no un-choosing now. This person's life and mine, this man and I, we can uncouple, but I can no longer opt out of his life.

In college, Taline and I went to DC with the rest of the Feminist Alliance to march on the anniversary of Roe v. Wade. Until recently, the most memorable part of that trip was the beginning, how the senior piloting the campus van got us stuck by driving the wrong way down a one-way street and a police officer had to come help us back out. I was mortified along with everyone else—we were supposed to be strong women who could drive a van! We all kicked in money for the ticket the officer issued when he returned our keys. For some reason, he gave them to Taline, who doesn't drive and was laughing so hard her eyes were tearing. Her laugh was infectious; I caught it. The senior snatched the keys back from her and we laughed even harder.

Thinking about the protest now, though, it is the march itself that comes into focus. Thousands of us, holding our signs and chanting with one voice. I know we were marching for people in many different situations: people whose pregnancies were unintended, unwanted, or dangerous. People whose pregnancies weren't viable or weren't at the right time. People like Isabel, who had trouble accessing her D&C after that dismal sixteen-week appointment. People like me. And who are people like me, exactly? I wish I knew. A pregnant person's choices and reasons—they're their own. Now the person with the choices is me.

Marc props his head up on a stack of decorative white eyelet pillows so he can see me from his side of the bed. "If we'd known that the move was already a fait accompli, we could have come out here in a month or two," he says. "When you felt better, and we could tell her. My grandma conned us."

"I think she had to," I say, closing my eyes, exhaustion tugging me under. "If she'd just asked us out for a visit, would we really have come?"

*

After our nap, we spend the afternoon going through a shoebox of old family photographs. Marc tries to convince Dinah to let us take the pictures with us to digitize, but she won't hear of it. "What if you lose them? What if you lose the disc you put them on?"

Marc loves all the glossy images of him as a baby. I know he's wondering if ours will look like him, hair swooping up in a cowlick, chin full of drool. We pass around a photo of Marc, ten months old or so, a fistful of spaghetti in one hand, a fork in the other, his face smeared with red sauce.

Marc is so sweet and thoughtful now, so scholarly and attentive, but from what I've heard, as a kid those qualities translated into *weird*. Instead of being the usual Star Wars, dinosaurs, and comic books kind of nerd, he got into classical music, epic poetry, and horticulture. A six-year-old asking Santa for fertilizer and pruning shears! As a girl, I was so middle-of-the-road, so normal, that I bored even myself. I'm still like that, I guess. Married to Marc and expecting. I don't want our baby to be like either of us.

Is that a normal thing to wish?

I accept a photo Marc passes me. "It was her first time going on an airplane," he says. Dinah is wearing a white—or light-colored, who can tell for sure with these black-and-white photographs?—skirt suit cinched with a belt at her trim waist, and a neat, narrow-brimmed hat tilted just so.

"That's how I looked boarding the plane at LaGuardia this morning, right?" I ask.

Dinah tries to throw this photo out, as she does with each and every one of herself—*What do I need a picture of me for?*—just to hear us argue back.

"Because you look like a movie star!"

"So we know where Marc gets his dimples from!"

"Because you look so *happy*!"

This last one gets a big eye roll. "Believe me when I say I have never been happier than I am right now," she tells us. "Now I do what I want to do, when I want to do it. Then? Psh."

All the photos go back in the box.

*

We head out for dinner at 5:15 p.m. Marc and I are fascinated by the idea of eating in the on-site cafeteria, but Dinah is adamant we don't even peek in through the glass doors on our way to the parking lot. "It's brisket night," she says, "which is always good. But my old table would want us to sit there so they could meet you—they've been hearing about you for years, Marc. And I passed around all the pictures from your wedding. They didn't understand your dress, Valerie—you know, why it was short and blue—but I told them to never mind. I don't sit there anymore, though, because of how Lucille acts when we play mahjong. They had different rules at the place where she used to live, and she won't adapt to how we do things here. We had a fight about it, so now I have to sit with Sol and them."

"Who is Sol?" I ask, but Dinah shakes her head at me, pressing her lips together. As we pass a line of elderly women sitting on benches on the patch of greenery between the building and the parking lot, they smile and nod at us, trying to slow us down. One of them even calls, "Is that your grandson, Dinah?" as Dinah waves her off and keeps walking to the car, besting both of us with her speed. I wonder whether Marc or I will bring up the fact that she's supposed to be in a wheelchair.

Marc helps Dinah into the front seat and pulls out a length of seat belt for her. "Are those friends from the old cafeteria table?" he asks.

"They talk too much," she says. "They'd want to ask a million questions that aren't their business. If we'd stopped, you would still be over there answering about why you haven't given me any great-grandbabies yet." Marc meets my eyes in the rearview. "*I'm* the only one who gets to ask you questions like that," she continues, tilting her head back with her dry, nearly soundless laugh. "But I won't, I won't."

Dinah directs us to a deli a few minutes' drive away. It has a cornflower-blue roof, OPEN glowing in pink neon over the swinging front door.

"I think I remember this place," Marc says. "Would we have gone here when I was a kid, Grandma?"

"Of course," she says. "You used to eat piles of liver and onions until one day, maybe you were ten, you stopped and asked, mouth full, 'Liver isn't real *livers*, right?' And then you leaned forward and spit it all out. A big, wet pile of chewed-up liver on the table. I thought it was funny, but your dad did not."

Marc and I bring down the average age of the deli clientele by decades. The waitress, herself not a young woman, seems to be delivering food to her tables without taking their orders. After we're seated, she hands us two menus, and a chocolate egg cream appears in front of Dinah.

"What can I get you?" she asks Marc and me.

"I think we need a minute with the menus," Marc says. "Are we the only ones in here who aren't regulars?"

"There's family and then there's family," she says.

Marc can't help himself; he beams across the table at me. He's fond of saying, now, that we're a family. He was always one for *we*, for *us*. He's been waiting since he was a kid, sitting with his plate of liver and onions, for this moment. I try to breathe through the desire to retreat outside to call Taline. What is it that makes me want to reach for her when Marc reaches for me?

The air is swirling with deli smells. A wave of pastrami hits me as a platter flies by to another table and I have to excuse myself to the bathroom, hustling to get there in time. After I throw up the few crumbs of cookie I'd managed earlier, throat raw and head throbbing, I feel diminished by at least 50 percent. Clenching my hands over my stomach, I wish I could already feel the baby in there instead of having to wait for something like ten more weeks. If evolution could have accomplished a concretization of this abstract future-child from the start, all-day, every day sickness would be easier to accept. But it's not a baby yet, that's the reality. It feels lonely because I'm alone here.

Leaning against the cool tile wall, I think back to that other dizzy day in a bathroom, pregnancy test in one hand, my phone and Taline's soothing voice in the other. She'd told me I needed to go to Marc, yes, but she also said, "You do know what to think, you know. I never tell you anything. All I do is listen so you can hear yourself."

When I return to the table, Marc looks anguished, but Dinah is placid, clearly at home here. "I ordered you an egg cream," she says. "Bubbles settle the stomach." She winks at me and my mouth sours again; what does she know? I glance at Marc, who appears immersed in his platter of stuffed cabbage.

Dinah is right, though: chocolate egg creams are magic. The stomach-coating dairy, the bubbles—I have two, leaving the kugel Marc chose for me mostly untouched on my plate. Dinah takes an eternity to finish one cheese-filled blintz. As she savors each bite, she tells us about Sol. "He got an electric wheelchair, but—typical—he didn't learn how to use it right," she says. "The day he brings it home, he rides into the lobby and—boom—he runs over two women. The next morning, he was back in the regular chair, an aide pushing him around."

I kick Marc under the table. He swallows his cabbage and kasha. "Grandma, we actually thought *you* were using a wheelchair now. That's why you moved to the first floor?"

Dinah puts down her fork. "Your father told you that?" She taps a long, pink-manicured nail on the table. "Let me ask you this. Do I seem like I need to use a wheelchair?"

We are silent, shaking our heads.

"When you get old," she says, "people stop listening to you. If they ever did to begin with. I was in a marriage for fifty-six years where I could have been delivering the Gettysburg Address and no one would have known it."

I nudge my straw around in my empty, milky glass.

"My kids learned from their father. I don't know how I could have done it differently, maybe it was just the time, but I wonder." She picks up her fork again, then puts it down and gestures for me to come closer. I scoot my chair and hold out my hand, but she reaches past it, reaches to touch my stomach. Her hand is cool, gentle, immovable. Marc's eyes flit to mine. He must have let the news slip, or at least confirmed her suspicions. He looks terrified that I've found him out.

"I've never been wrong," Dinah says. "All the rushing to the bathroom, that glassy look in your eyes? Don't be mad at him for telling me. I knew, I knew the moment I saw you."

I am faint for a moment, reorienting to the room, to a world in which this information is on the outside, not just a small internal pulse only for me, Taline, Marc, and the doctor.

Hand still on my belly, Dinah turns to Marc. "You tell your daughter," she says. "You tell her to listen when her mother talks, okay?"

Maybe she's right about this, too. Maybe we will have a daughter. Maybe she'll be blond when she's born, like Marc. Maybe she'll be quick and sharp, like Dinah. Maybe she'll be, somehow, like me.

"You'll tell her that?" I ask Marc, although as soon as I ask, I know he will. There is no mystery to Marc. I try another bite of kugel.

Dinah's palm is still on my stomach and, along with the morning sickness, another feeling starts to swell somewhere beneath the surface: anticipation. I want to meet this new person. She is growing as we sit at this table together: eyes, a spine, ten tiny toes. In just a few weeks, she'll be able to hear. I'll say to her, Baby, there is so much you already know.

DAY JOBS
Taline, 2008

THE GROUP OF US ARE WEDGED INTO AND ONTO EVERY COUCH, corner, and cushion in this musty Upper West Side living room. Reece and I, sharing a carpet square, are squeezed beside a low-slung coffee table; my knees bang every time I squirm or shift. There is a bowl of green grapes we keep passing around although there are not nearly enough for everyone. "Taline," Reece whispers. "Do you think those were left over from Ophira's lunch?"

I pop one in my mouth; it is warm. Its flesh separates around my molars like something animal. "Likely," I say.

Across the room, one of the dancers is breastfeeding her baby. I remember from our last meeting that he's named after an island. Borneo sticks in my head, but I don't think that's it. Bali? Her areola is large, much larger than mine. I often find myself thinking about this when I see women breastfeeding. Is it the baby that does it? Valerie's baby is coming soon; she'll want to know if this is the case. Reece has kids, so I make a mental note to ask her when the meeting is over. Although that time may not come for a while. It's five minutes past when we're supposed to have started and Ophira, our boss, owner of this apartment-cum-makeshift conference space, is still over in the kitchen. I can hear her Brooklyn vowels but not the words they round out.

One of the musicians, a deeply sexy percussionist named Isaac, is rapping his thumbs on the coffee table. He is ageless in his drop-crotch pants and thin black sweater. He has what looks like a hemp rope tied in a giant loop around his neck. If I could watch anyone else in here teach, it would be him.

An opera singer—imposing, purple-clad—leans over and asks, "You two new?"

"This is Taline's third year, my sixth," Reece explains. "We're visual artists."

But the singer's already lost interest.

Being the visual artists in this group translates to a certain kind of invisibility. Everyone else is a performer and they perform accordingly. Even though we're all teaching artists with Solid Starts Through the Arts—acronymed SSTARTS—we only get together every few months, hence the lack of an actual meeting room. Usually we're deployed separately, sharing our particular art forms in public schools that don't otherwise have access. Everyone else leads with their bodies and their big personalities. Reece and I write lesson plans and link them to state learning standards. I guess I'm not sure if that's our discipline or something more innate. No one really talks to us at these meetings.

Luckily the kids like us, and that's what matters. The way Reece puts it is this: "They walk into the room and talk; we walk in and listen."

Not that our colleagues are all bad. There's a performance artist whose wiry arms are always exposed and who invites us to her one-woman shows. The capoeira practitioner who greets us with double kiss-kisses on each cheek. And there's Isaac, of course. Reece and I became friends my first year after a long day at a middle school. I was shadowing her as part of my training. I loved her way with the students: so respectful and thoughtful. She challenged them and made them laugh. I took copious notes. We had five back-to-back classes that day; I observed the first two, assisted with the second two, and taught the fifth myself. The kids were full of insight and ideas and *energy*. At the end of the day, we were wiped out. We were bonded. So, after our next meeting, even though it was only three in the afternoon, she accepted my invitation to go grab a drink. A few mojitos in, she started talking about Isaac's hands, and I admitted I'd done some thinking about those hands, too.

The room is beginning to smell, like people, or the sour edge of the grapes. This meeting isn't only starting late but was pushed back three weeks; it is already October. We have a small but loyal core of schools that keeps us busy and employed; we're anxious, after the summer, to start the cash flowing—or *trickling* might be more accurate—again.

Finally, Ophira enters the room. She has gray hair plaited in two long braids and a wardrobe that incorporates a lot of crushed velvet. Her glasses, wire-rimmed, spend most of their time at the tip of her nose. We love Ophira and Ophira loves us. She says her job is twofold—to bring the arts into the schools and to bring paychecks to the artists. She herself plays the flute.

Following behind her is a woman in a suit. The woman belongs in a boardroom, not here among us bohemians. Her clothes fit so well. She's like Hillary Clinton, almost, in how she wears a pants suit. With the election coming up, I think about Hillary a lot. Not that I'm not excited to vote for Obama. I voted for him in the primary. Val jokingly blamed me when he won, as if it were my vote that tipped it.

The baby is mewling, and the opera singer is holding forth about something, so it takes Ophira a moment to direct everyone's attention to the woman. "This is . . . well, some of you may know her," she starts, then trails off, swallowing hard before resuming her introduction. "This is our director, Calais."

I can picture her name on my pay stub—Calais Saint-Yves. What a beautiful name! everyone must exclaim when they meet her. I've never seen her in the flesh. She works in SSTARTS' midtown administrative office; the only time I've been there was for my interview. Calais's hair is blond and coiffed, her super-shiny silver drop earrings tasteful but also, just a little, cool.

"It is good to see you all," Calais begins. "You are, of course, the backbone of this organization. Your talents are tremendous, and your dedication to the schoolchildren of New York City is profound."

I'm nodding along, finding it all innocent enough until Reece clamps her hand on my thigh. "Shit," she whispers. I glance around and see everyone's faces going queasy.

Calais pauses. She looks to Ophira. Ophira looks at her feet. We all look at each other. "That's why, well, that's why Ophira invited me here to talk to you all about this. As you may or may not know," she says, clearing her already clear throat, "our major source of funding was Lehman Brothers."

I get this feeling, while she's explaining, that this is my fault, karmically speaking. I'd felt smug, last month, watching those fuckers on the news, carrying their cardboard boxes out onto the street. That's what you get, I'd thought. What were you doing for the world?

For being the voice of professional reason, Calais isn't any better at this than Ophira would have been herself. She isn't crying, but she's speaking in tongues, in strange corporate speak like the kind that probably got the country into this mess.

My eyes and Isaac's catch, like his are a key and mine are a latch—they stay locked like that as he asks, "Have we lost our jobs? Is that it, then?"

His eyes are amber, swirling with gold and brown. I almost lose track of the answer to his question, but luckily Ophira's stuck on repeat: "No," she says. "No, no."

We all sigh. Then she says, "But."

She turns it back to Calais, who goes on to explain one of the wildest solutions to a nonprofit crisis I have ever heard, and having been a teaching artist in various organizations for years now, that's saying something. I've been furloughed, worked for four months without a paycheck, stolen supplies from one job to use at another, and taught *theater* when the theater teacher went MIA. Little surprises me. But.

"There are two of you in every discipline. Now, with our funding so diminished, we can only pay one," she says. Reece and I look to each other, stricken. "But we would like to leave it up to you. Either one of you stays and the other explores new opportunities, or you both stay with halved salaries."

"We don't get salaries," Isaac says. I like how he makes sure that point doesn't lie. I wish I had the confidence to speak up like he does; I wish I had the confidence of a man in a room full of women. We get paid per program we teach, nothing in the event of a snow day. I think of my ex-boyfriend and his tenure-track job upstate. Me and my half degree, we've yet to find a more reliable source of income in our chosen field. I'd called the continuing ed program at the community college by my mom, thinking maybe I could get the gig Jeremiah used to have, and I found out it paid even worse than SSTARTS, and there were no openings anyway. I keep expecting my days of three roommates and accepting checks from my mom will come to an end soon, that I'm closer and closer to figuring out a career, a place for myself in the city. I'm on the verge of feeling sorry for myself, but then I look around the room and get a grip.

"Half your fee," Calais clarifies. I get the sense that she could lose her job and be just fine. She has a moneyed look, a remove.

The performance artist stands up and bows to her actor counterpart. "All yours," she says. "Jesus." She breezes out of the room. Ophira watches her go with bright, watery eyes.

"Wait, are we deciding now?" Reece asks. Her lean, usually lineless face is pinched.

Ophira hangs her head low, catching her glasses with one hand as they tumble off. "Take a few days," she says, surveying the room. She is the kind of boss who makes sure to look us all in the eye. "I just couldn't choose. You are all so special."

Isaac and the other musician, a guy who goes by Frogger, play together when they're not teaching. They're turned toward the corner, whispering. The baby's head is lolling around as the dancer packs him into the wrap around her middle; he's sleeping so hard he doesn't notice he's getting jostled around.

"To be able to sleep like that," Ophira says. She doesn't say anything else, so we all stand up to leave.

*

Outside, Reece says, "That Calais woman was useless."

"She does work here, too," I say. "That doesn't say much for her competence."

Reece shakes her head. "I keep thinking, what if King Solomon was like—no, *you* cut the baby in half."

We head straight for a Chinese restaurant down the block that serves tiki drinks, where we sit at a table in the window and order scorpion bowls. "These are for two people," the server says. "So, you want one?"

"We want two," I say, and she frowns but brings them. They are sugar and fire. "Spring break senior year, I did a flaming shot and frizzled my bangs," I tell Reece. "I always had my hair hanging in front of my face. It was like my trademark. Then, boom, gone. Everyone thought it was hilarious."

"Well, wasn't it?" Reece asks, and I have to admit that yes, probably it was. But I can tell from the edge in her voice that we might have a problem. Reece lived with her grandmother during college, half boarder, half caretaker; she didn't spend four years going to parties and changing majors like I did.

"Let's just drink these before we talk about the job," Reece says, swirling her maraschino cherry around in her murky drink. "What's going on in the studio?"

I plunge my straw to the bottom of the bowl, sucking up the heavy pineapple juice that's settled there. "Color fields," I say. "Abstract, but scaled to my body. I used to fixate on my hips, how they were too wide, how my stomach was too soft. I had this summer school art teacher; even when our class was over, I'd send him pictures of my work and he'd give me feedback. He said I 'skinnified' myself in my self-portraits. It always mortified me that he said that, but it was true. Anyway, I'm trying to make a different kind of self-portrait. To take up space. But can I even afford to work like that now?"

"You have a lot to say. You'll find a way to say it."

"And you?" I ask.

"Breasts," she says. "I thought I was making these ceramic vessels about landmass. Taking clay from the land and re-creating the land. Then, my kid takes one look and says, 'Boobs again, Mama?'" She laughs. "And I just had to say, 'Boobs again.'"

"That reminds me," I ask. "Does the areola get larger when you breastfeed?"

"That dancer is a special case," she says. "Why, you worried?"

"God no," I say, shuddering. "My best friend is about to have a baby, and she told me there actually isn't enough room in your body for the baby and your lungs?" As I recount this conversation, I realize we had it weeks ago. Whenever I invite Val to do something with me, she says she's on deadline. She'll call me sometimes, but if I call her, the phone just rings. I think she's avoiding me because she's still mad I left her in Austin. But we're both in New York now—why keep missing each other when we don't have to?

"I remember that feeling," Reece says, crushing an ice cube between her teeth. "Like constant suffocation. But you like kids. You signed up for this circus."

"Sure, I love kids," I say.

"Aren't you seeing someone?" Reece asks. "The cop?"

"Oh," I say. "I can't believe I told you about that."

Reece reaches over to tap my glass with her nail. I must have been drinking if I'd admitted to her that I was sleeping with a police officer. She raises her eyebrows at me, waiting for more.

"I keep swearing I won't go over there again. I mean, it's only happened three or four times, when I'm in Jersey visiting my mom. Last time, I said that was it. But he's a cop. He doesn't really hear the word no, you know?" I cover my face with my hand, remembering how Colin had smashed his drink down on the table when I suggested maybe this thing with us had run its course. How he'd grabbed my waist and pulled me toward him, like usual but just that much rougher. How I let him.

"Oh, I know," Reece says.

That's it, I think. Don't return his calls.

She continues, "You're not ready to settle down. Those big canvases. It's still all about you."

"I don't know if that's it." When I start feeling the drink, it's in the form of a headache, a throb right between my eyes.

Should I tell her she can have the job? I love this job. I don't want to, but should I bow out?

We are startled by a *knock-knock-knock*ing on the window. Through the tinted glass I see glimmers of daylight and Isaac. He and Frogger pause, squint, enter the restaurant. We all re-introduce ourselves, although only two of us need to assimilate the information. Isaac slides in next to Reece, leaving Frogger to settle beside me. He's wearing a strange outfit—gray flannel pants, gray flannel shirt, motorcycle jacket. I can't tell if it is interesting or just bizarre. His hair is parted down the middle and pulled into a ponytail; he smells like leather.

"You two have the right idea," he says, waving over the server, ordering a couple of Heinekens. "Chinese restaurants always have Heineken," he adds after she walks away.

"I think it has something to do with a certain region in the north. I read an article explaining why once," I say. Everyone looks at me expectantly. "I actually can't remember the reason."

"Speaking of," Isaac says, "you notice Sherry wasn't here today? That phone call is going to be quite the surprise."

In the pause that follows, I suspect we're all remembering the meeting a few months ago when Sherry, a dancer from China, announced she had become an American citizen. She thanked Ophira for the job, which had helped make it happen. We were all wiping our eyes. It was that she stood up to share the news that was so moving. I swear it was the first time in my life I'd ever felt patriotic.

The beers arrive. Isaac and I toast first, then clink with Reece and Frogger.

"You know," Isaac says, "I used to be a banker. In another life."

"Can you picture this man in a suit?" Frogger asks. I can, but that's beside the point.

"I'm shocked," I say, although his acumen at the meeting clicks now. "How did you find your way back from the dark side?"

As he laughs, I can see the soft pink of his throat.

"My high school had an internship program for the kids who were smart but a pain in the ass to keep in the building all day. Up until that point, I'd sort of made a career of correcting my teachers, pissing them off. So, they sent me to Wall Street. Somehow it made sense to me. I was intimidated as fuck, maybe, so I actually listened when people spoke. Surprise, surprise, I could learn something that way. I was good enough that when I graduated, I went to City College part time, worked down on Wall Street the other half. Paid my way through school and then some."

Is it my imagination, or is he staring right at me? All the while, his hands have been doing a silent tap dance on his place mat, keeping beat with his story. "You make it sound noble," I say. I feel like we're on a date, a date where I can hear someone else swallowing beside me and a girlfriend is kicking me under the table.

Frogger interrupts. "You know the rest, ladies. He feels creatively unfulfilled, wants to make a real difference, quits to play music and work with kids. Give the man a medal."

"What about you?" Reece asks, turning her kind attention to Frogger. I get the sense she's doing it half to be polite, half to make me tear my gaze away from Isaac.

"I came up through a conservatory and am real good, but not quite good enough to be the one guy playing clarinet in the few places folks pay you to play clarinet. Maybe because I couldn't ever focus, played too many instruments. I'm a man who loves too much." He elbows me in the side; I give him his laugh.

There are four beer bottles on the table. "Did you each drink two already?" I ask. "Where was I?"

Isaac nods toward the empty fishbowl in front of me. My stomach churns, the first stirrings of heartburn.

"I've noticed, gentlemen," Reece says, "that as enlightened as you are—musicians, teachers of young children—you call us ladies. You tell your life stories but don't ask us ours."

Isaac narrows his eyes, his mouth half a smirk. "We'll get there," he says.

But Frogger unleashes a stream of apologies. He concludes with, "I hope you can appreciate that I'm a little distracted by the events of the meeting today."

"No shit," Reece says.

"I couldn't stop thinking of King Solomon when Ophira was talking," Isaac says, and Reece exclaims, dropping her hand onto his, "Taline, didn't I say the exact same thing?"

"You did," I concede. "Ophira's relying on us to be too nice to cause a problem." I glance between Reece's ring and her eyes. I won't mention that she's married. Not aloud at least. "Splitting one job between two people is stupid. But it's not like we're going to duel for the job."

"I'd duel," Frogger says, brandishing an empty beer bottle. Isaac grabs one, too, and they *clink, clink, clink.*

"Let's duel," Isaac says. "It's a good idea. Let's go head-to-head."

I hold up my hands, abdicating responsibility. I feel my brain still moving after my face has stopped.

"We can probably get lawyers involved here," Reece says. "Asking us to make this decision can't possibly be legal."

Isaac and Frogger scoff.

"I guess these guys really want to fight," I say. "Should we convince them violence isn't the answer?"

Isaac's not looking at me anymore, but right at Frogger.

The duel has already begun.

*

Isaac and Frogger share a rehearsal space. We take a cab there. Frogger sits up front with the driver and I'm psyched about how Isaac's knee presses against mine until I see his other one is equally as cozy with Reece's.

Their space is about the size of a walk-in closet. It's soundproofed and instantly warm with four people crowded inside. It seems like everyone else has started to sober up, so it's up to me to name the rules for the duel, to keep the revelry—if that's what this is—going.

"Reece and I will sit here," I say. "And each of you has three minutes to play for us. Show us your souls. Play for your lives."

Frogger bites his lower lip. "We play the same instrument?"

"Your choice," I say. "Play whatever will make us fall in love."

He rubs the knuckles of one hand along the palm of his other. "That's not really fair," he says. "And I think you know why."

"Don't be a pussy," Reece says. I am not the only one still feeling my drink, it seems.

We slide down the wall onto the floor. Isaac says, "I'll go first."

Frogger opens his mouth as if to argue, but then closes it again and joins us on the ground. I'm both a little giddy and a little dizzy. Reece tips to the side so she can whisper into my ear: "This is nuts." I wink.

Instruments hang on the walls and cover all the surfaces in the room. Isaac selects a thumb piano, which I remember him explaining at a meeting is also called an mbira, eight thin metal tines on a wooden board shaped like, or maybe made from, a round yellow gourd. He sits on a wooden stool with one leg a little shorter than the others, the mbira on his lap. His left hand starts with the bass, his right with the melody. His eyes flit between Reece and me, playing us as much as the instrument. His fingers are tapering and fast. Each note he plucks causes a vibration, a ripple effect. Each note splits and multiplies. I'm about to call time when three minutes is up but Frogger beats me to it. We clap; Reece hoots.

When he and Isaac trade places, Isaac whispers into my ear, "So did I win?" and I feel his breath on my face.

"My therapist will not be pleased that I am engaging with this," Frogger says, taking his position in front of us, his smile wry. "She says I often subject myself to humiliation. She has pointed out that the name I go by, even, is a sign that I see myself as the butt of a joke."

"What's your real name?" Reece asks.

Ignoring her, he licks his lips and begins to play his clarinet.

My eyes wander up to the ceiling, where the plaster is missing in places, exposing wooden beams underneath. The fine white film covering the floor must drift down from there. It's like snow falling, the slips of light from the studio upstairs shining through the missing ceiling, their missing floor, like the smallest glimpse of space, the stars, heaven. I realize when my thoughts grow rhapsodic that it's the music doing it. I look back at Frogger and he's lost, too. Reece's eyes are closed, listening. Even Isaac is following the music, his hands on his knees. Wherever Frogger is when he plays, he's not the butt of anyone's joke.

No one calls time. We let him play and play. It's like we don't even come to until he stops himself, until a moment or so after.

I start to laugh. What beauty there is in the world! What a relief, what a release!

Reece and I both look to Isaac. I expect him to say, "It's yours, man." But he, now, is the one looking at his hands.

"Well?" Frogger asks. He doesn't know. He doesn't know how good he is.

Isaac doesn't look up.

"Frogger," I say, "it's you."

*

Reece's apartment is within walking distance from their space, so we wait on the sidewalk as she packs up one of her pieces. I know I'm messed up because I can't tell what the weather is like. Am I cold? The light is fading. "I'm never in Harlem," I say, looking around me at the brick and brownstones.

Isaac claps his hands. "You don't say."

His feelings are hurt. His feelings and his pride. I want to point out that none of this is binding, that the duel idea was a joke, but who am I to point anything out at this point? The white girl who's never in Harlem and still receives checks from her mom four times a year. The white girl who sleeps with a cop and still thinks about Hillary.

Reece returns with a cardboard box in her arms. Isaac tries to take it, but she swats him away. "I don't trust anyone but me with this," she says. "In fact, I don't even trust me. I'm not a big day drinker."

"It's the end times," Isaac says. "We are headed straight into the Great Depression part two. Right back to the Dust Bowl."

"I showed that photograph to a class once," Reece says, "you know the one. The kids wanted to know where the daddy was. I kept saying, 'But let's talk about the mom, the one who is there.' They couldn't get past it."

"I read that family turned out fine," I say. "They got through it."

Reece looks at me like I am one of her students, maybe one of her kids. It is a *stop* kind of look. I can see myself, for a moment, in a way I usually can't. I'm losing Isaac, that's for sure. He and Reece, if I'm being honest, seem to be exchanging looks. Am I losing her?

She says, "Speaking of family . . ." She balances her box on her hip and takes out her phone. She's got to find someone to fetch her kids from afterschool. "This shit is going to go past five."

My crowning achievement, the best thing I've ever done, was to apply for and receive a subsidized studio on the Lower

East Side. It's in a former public school subdivided into spaces for what seems like half the other visual artists in New York. The windows are large, the ceilings are high, and no one balks when I bust out a power tool. We trudge single file down the hall. Reece asks to go in first to set up her work. I let her, because Frogger has gone off to pee.

Alone with Isaac, in the dark echo of the hallway, I ask, "How much do you actually care about this job?"

"Probably about as much as you do," he says, which doesn't answer my question. I lean back and feel the smooth paint and the divots of the cinderblock behind me. I wonder if there's anything I could do to make him like me.

Reece cracks the door. "Ready," she says. Frogger rounds the corner, and we all enter at once. Despite everything else, I feel a swell of pride, seeing my work greeting us. I don't have anywhere to stash away my paintings, so they're all on display by default, leaning against the walls. I've been using a coarse, industrial canvas, leaving it unprimed. It lets light through in uneven, cloudlike patches. In places where the canvas is particularly nubby, the color is intensified, like firefly flickers or sparks.

Reece has draped the small table I use to support my palette with one of my drop cloths, creating a sort of pedestal. Her sculpture atop the stand is about eight inches high, a foot across, and yes, it looks like a breast. Sturdy, yet tender. It is unglazed except for certain small stretches where it almost looks polished. The men rotate around it, taking it in. I haven't seen much of her work before; I think it's pretty good.

"I like how your fingerprints are in it," Isaac says.

"It's sexy," Frogger adds. "But also creepy."

Reece smiles, pleased. "I can live with sexy-creepy. Better than creepy-sexy."

They both scan the room, taking in my canvases. Frogger seems to linger on my new blue work. Then he asks, "Where's yours, Taline?"

I'm quiet for a moment. Is he serious? It's not that he doesn't see the work—of course he does. I wait. Is he trying to be mean? But Isaac turns around, and then around again. Searching, too. They just don't know it's art.

Reece is the one who gestures. "Oh," they say. "Oh, oh."

"I was going to say that I shouldn't quit my day job." I reach for a piece of canvas and pluck a thread free. "But I guess I just did."

The way we're standing, me and Isaac facing Reece and Frogger across the room, we're divided into winners and losers.

"Let's all quit," Frogger says. "This was unfair, and we can find other work. Let's all give our notice." He's being kind. I'm not sure, but I think it may be obvious to all of us: Frogger is the real artist here.

Maybe Isaac will go back to banking. Those jobs will return first, before the jobs like ours, that much goes without saying.

Reece begins to pack up her sculpture again. The sun has disappeared behind the low downtown buildings. The room is dusky and cold.

I open the studio door. They all start to file out, Isaac first, then Reece. She gives me a fast, tight hug, but averts her eyes.

I grab Frogger's shirt as he is about to pass me. He jerks back, eyebrows raised, expectant. He wants, I think, for me to absolve him. There's no way to hide that he just broke my heart. But he shouldn't feel bad for being better. Maybe he's in an even worse spot: having a real gift but nowhere to put it. He leans in to hug me, and I don't hug back. The door closes behind him.

*

There are a few half-melted candles scattered about the studio. I use them sometimes when I want to set a contemplative mood. I pick up one, beeswax-colored, citrus-scented. I dig around the blackened wick with my fingernail and light it. I catch a drop of molten wax on my fingertip and roll it into a ball. I tilt the flame toward the nearest canvas. At first, nothing happens. It licks upward: yellow, orange, red. I move it closer. A whisp of smoke coils toward the ceiling. The canvas singes and the colors deepen. Maybe I'm onto something. A little closer. Yellow. Orange. Red. Yellow. Orange. Red. Then, wow. Look at them go.

SHALLOW LATCH
Valerie, 2008

"I didn't even know she'd been born," I tell Louise, dear Louise, who'd arrived at the apartment with six croissants and two coffees, both for me. That she brought breakfast told me it was still morning, but I saw the grapefruit glow of sunrise so long ago I would have guessed it was much later.

"You must have passed out," she says as I use one hand to extract a cashmere hoodie from a gift bag she gives me. I'm learning how to do everything this way, lopsided, only a single limb my own at any point. I hold the baby in the crook of my other arm, which is balanced across my lap because I can barely feel it, I've been holding her so long. We've accumulated a lot of darling onesies and sleepers, but Louise is the only person who's brought something just for me. I rub the soft sweater against my cheek. Louise has on jeans and a T-shirt, an outfit I would have worn mere months ago but seems completely out of reach now. I'm wearing the same pajamas I've had on since what might have been Thursday. Without sleep to separate the days, it is hard to know.

I pick the chocolate out of my second pastry and flick a buttery flake off the baby's funny, peeling forehead. "Did you know babies molt like, like snakes?" I ask. "The skin they had in the womb peels off. No one told me that." Louise cringes; she hates snakes. Back when I still worked for her, one of the designers proposed a line of animal print tights and Louise couldn't nix it fast enough.

"Sorry! Bad metaphor," I say. "And no, I didn't pass out. It had been going on so long that I'd sort of convinced myself it would never end. That the pain was forever and so I had to start living with it. It was a way to cope. I forgot that there was a goal in mind. I had a cold compress over my eyes and was hyperventilating no matter how many times the nurses told me to breathe, and I couldn't stop crying and just thought, This is my life now. This is eternity. Then Marc was pulling the cloth from my face, and everyone was yelling, 'Open your eyes, Valerie, open your eyes!' I was surprised to see her there. The baby, I mean."

"And then what?" Louise tucks around her thighs a beige-and-white knit blanket my great-aunt had sent for the baby. It is chilly in the apartment. That we have no control over our thermostat has always been a nuisance, but now I wonder: Will the lack of heat, then the sudden 3 a.m. blasting heat, kill the baby?

Louise pumps a bit of Purell on her hands and extends them. I give her the baby, who does a kitten stretch and makes an alarming grimace, then settles back down.

I feel buoyant lifting the coffee cup, my biceps unburdened of the baby's eight pounds for the first time in hours.

She won't be put down, this baby, not even to sleep. For the first few days, I was so scared I'd drop her that I didn't sleep at all and just sat on the couch holding her, wishing I could put her back inside, where she was clearly more comfortable. Where she'd been safe. I never would have thought that those forty weeks—why do people say nine months? Forty weeks is longer than that—with sciatica and the around-the-clock nausea, the piercing headaches and the wicked leg cramps, I never would have thought that was the easy part. Around day five after she was born, my scalp twitching from sleeplessness, I passed out in that way where I had no idea I was asleep until I woke up an hour later. I have been sleeping on occasion since then and haven't dropped her yet. I gulp from the paper cup, the coffee warming me from my throat on down. How does even drinking coffee feel different now? Some women give up caffeine when they're breastfeeding, like martyrs. Please.

"I shouldn't tell you this," I say. "It's so gross. I was numb from the epidural—even though they turned it off when it was time to push because it was making it so I didn't feel the urge to push and that was a problem and so I felt it, I felt every bit of those four hours when her hand was next to her face blocking her own exit—but for some reason, they needed me to pee right after she was born, and so this nurse, truly the most saintly person I've ever met, helped me to the bathroom. I wasn't sure if I was peeing or not, and it turns out I wasn't, and it was a whole to-do. That's something I really truly won't give you the details on. But she helped me up from the toilet and I glanced down and—Louise, I really shouldn't tell you this either."

I pause, giving her the chance to tell me to go on. Years ago, when I needed to buy a car, I had no idea how to go about getting one. Louise took me to a used car dealership on Northern Boulevard in Queens. I stood frozen in the face of all the cars, knowing only which one looked the prettiest. "You want a Honda Civic," Louise said. "Driving across the country? That'll get you there." She asked the guy in the sharp shiny suit for the Carfax and cited the blue book; the only blue book I knew was the academic kind I scribbled my test answers in. That car carried me to Texas and back; we brought the baby home from the hospital in it; and if I had to guess, it is where my husband is taking a quick nap in the grocery store parking lot as we speak. Even when it isn't to her benefit—she literally helped me leave a job where my whole role was helping her!—Louise always comes through. But now she says, "Okay, okay, don't tell me."

I rub my eyes to bring her into focus. She doesn't mean it. How can I stop here?

"Everywhere," I say. "The blood! Like, the floor. My legs. Everywhere. Still now, fifteen days later. Every time I move, even, there's more. I didn't know a person could lose so much blood and still, you know. Live."

*

I'm in the shower, warm washcloths—a super-soft organic kind meant for the baby—folded over both cracked nipples, breathing the steam. Louise is with the baby so I'm taking longer than usual, the new usual. Last time I showered, the baby was in the bathroom with me, strapped into her despised bouncer and screaming so frantically that I couldn't even manage long enough to rinse the shampoo fully from my hair. Now I want to relax, but the patter of the water on the mildewed tiles takes on the nagging rhythm of all these two-word terms I can't get out of my head:

Back labor.

Cluster feeding.

Shallow latch.

Moro reflex.

Marc and I took a six-week childbirth class and didn't hear a peep about any of them, but days into parenthood, they became all too familiar. Single words, too:

Bleb.

Supplement.

Reflux.

Swaddle.

Then, that terrible alliteration:

Baby blues.

Baby blues.

Baby blues.

Before having the baby, I'd heard someone say that the best feeling in the world is turning off the shower and hearing silence, as in, not hearing the baby crying, and I'd thought that seemed like a sad best feeling to have. Up until now, some best feelings:

Reading *Sense and Sensibility* for the first time.

Ordering and eating an entire pizza, crust and all.

Floating on my back in the bracing ocean surf, the summer sun beating down on my upturned face.

The first sip of a very cold, very lime-y gin and tonic.

My mother's proud, teary smile at my wedding.

Eyes fluttering open in the middle of the night, checking the clock, and seeing that I don't have to be awake for hours still. Hours of still.

Finally, the water starts to run cool. I twist the handles; the steam dwindles in an instant:

the baby is crying.

*

Cleaner than I've been in days, I hurry to wiggle into my stretchy hospital-issue disposable underwear and a pad before I bleed all over the floor. I zip up the luxurious hoodie with nothing under it and pull on some old sweatpants. The baby's quieted down to a whimper, so I take a second to stop and brush my teeth. My gums bleed like crazy now, too, another fun fact no one thought to mention before it started to happen. It feels amazing to brush my teeth, though. Throughout my pregnancy the smell of mint churned my stomach, but as soon as the baby was born, that changed—one of the few changes that's been for the better. I was used to turning away from Marc's minty goodnight kisses, but the day after we got home from the hospital, suddenly it was fine. I actually enjoyed the kiss.

But then he fell asleep, and I was up all night with the baby. We'd agreed to take turns, but why would I wake him when all the baby wanted was milk? How could he possibly help? I'd spent so many years reading and analyzing texts that reject biological determinism, interrogate ideas of what is natural, and deconstruct our assumptions about traditional gender roles and reveal them to be cultural, societal, and rooted in the patriarchy, but at 4 a.m. the fact remains that I'm the one with the milk. If I want Marc to take a middle-of-the-night feeding, or if Marc wants to take a middle-of-the-night feeding, I'll either have to pump to get him the bottle to feed her with, or use formula and still have to pump after to keep up my milk supply and also because it hurts not to and that'll take even longer than just nursing her to begin with and and and.

I step out into the hall and pause. I hear voices. Is Marc home? It doesn't sound like Marc. Then I remember: Taline. Did I really tell her and Louise to come at the same time? Is today Sunday? I practically break into a run. She'd planned to come to the hospital, but she picked up a stomach bug in some classroom or another. In the living room, she leaps from the couch, grabs me, and squeezes. It hurts everywhere, but I don't say that. I'm crying and so is she.

"You had a baby!" she says.

I wipe my eyes, looking for her. The baby. "Oh," I say. "Louise still has her."

"Yeah," says Taline. "We met. She's amazing."

"We all met," says Louise.

Everything is so new, so weird, that it takes a moment to put together that Louise and Taline have never met. They would have at my wedding, but Marc and I got married so soon after we were engaged—partly because we got a deal on the venue after another couple canceled on short notice, partly so I wouldn't have time to change my mind—and Louise was already booked to speak at a conference. It's only been the last few months we've all been in the same city, just the pregnant months, mostly, when I was working overtime, puking, and choosing paint colors. The baby is so small in Louise's arms, I wonder how she could have displaced so much already.

"I didn't mean to invite you both at the same time," I say. "I am a bit scattered." It's almost as if a double life is being revealed, as if I have two separate families, secret to each other. It shouldn't feel like that, though. Taline and Louise know about each other. They have from the start. But aren't groups of three hard? I remember from childhood—playdates in trios end in tears. Someone is always left out.

Also, Louise knows too much. I don't know why I thought it was a good idea to complain about Taline to her, as if this would never happen. As soon as Taline told me that she and Alex broke up, a mere seven seconds after she left me alone in Texas to be with him, I texted Louise a series of very uncharitable emojis about it.

But Louise says to her, "I'm glad we're finally meeting. It's about time, right?" and it sounds genuine. It hits me that all that complaining, if it reflects poorly on anyone, it's probably me. Louise knows better. She extends her arms toward Taline. "Do you want to hold her now?" The baby's unfocused eyes are at half-mast. To me Louise says, "Taline didn't want to take her until you were out."

"It felt wrong," Taline says.

"By all means!" I say, but then, as if at my voice, the baby begins to scream again, a real zero-to-sixty situation. Does she really know me? I slide onto the couch beside Louise. Taline sits on my other side. "Sorry," I say. "I guess she has other ideas."

I shift and struggle and switch seats with Taline so my arm is propped up on the couch, trying to get into a nursing position that's comfortable for both me and the baby. I have three different kinds of pillows that are supposed to help but don't. Finally, I wrestle her into what the lactation consultant called the "football hold" and she latches. I feel the brief but searing pain of my milk letting down. Then she's nursing. The hard part, for the moment, is over, so I try to remember how to ask my friends about themselves. I don't want anyone feeling excluded. I must have succeeded in posing a question because Louise says, "My brother and Céleste had their engagement party last night." I know that, somewhere inside me, I am excited about this. I smile and nod, trying to excavate something of that excitement. To Taline, Louise explains, "Céleste is this utterly perfect creature who has, for some reason, agreed to marry my goofy brother. She's French, she's beautiful, and she's got her shit *so* together. At family functions, I'm an absolute ogre in comparison."

Taline looks skeptical. Next to the two of us, Louise is all the things she just mentioned and more. Not French, of course, but beautiful, composed, and successful. I can't tell if Taline is charmed that Louise doesn't see herself that way or appalled. I'll try to remember to tell her later that this isn't false modesty, it's just how she is.

I should say something to Taline now. Go ahead, I tell myself. "Taline is an artist," I tell Louise, although this is probably one of the few things she already knows. "How is . . . your art?"

A funny look crosses Taline's face. "I had a bit of a problem. A mistake," she says. We wait for her to continue, which she seems reticent to do. "Well, I tried to burn my canvases. Just to see what would happen. To see how it would look." She grimaces. "Anyway, I got kicked out of the studio."

It takes me a moment to process. "You're saying you set a fire?" I switch the baby to the other side, flinch as she re-latches, and try to picture Taline's beautiful color fields going up in flames. "On purpose?"

Taline flushes. "I tried to burn them," she says. "That's not really the same thing as setting a fire. But it wasn't my best idea. It got a little out of hand."

"Are you okay?" asks Louise. I glance at her. That was a better question to ask.

"It's for the best," Taline says. She smiles like it's all fine, but I know her. I may be a shell of myself, but I can tell she's being evasive. That line about burning being different than setting a fire?

Then I notice the baby has her eyes closed. No, I think, no, no, no. I need a cold seltzer from the kitchen. I ask Louise to go get it. It could be a two-birds-with-one-stone situation—there is a lot of information I should be trying to extract from Taline in Louise's absence—but the baby needs to wake up. She needs to eat. When Louise returns with the can, I hold it to the back of the baby's neck as she nurses, turning it when she needs a new burst of cold to keep her awake. "It's the only time she wants to sleep," I say. My voice wavers. Why does this feel like such a big deal? Is this a big deal? "When she needs to eat, she gets on the boob and passes out. Then I try to move, and she screams because she's hungry. She can't sleep because it'll ruin her sleep."

"What a jerk," Taline says. We all laugh. Maybe it's not a big deal. Maybe it's funny. She tries to add something about when Zoe had a newborn but suddenly can't get a word out. I've changed positions slightly, which causes the baby to spit up. Sour milk projectiles across the front of my new sweater. And now she is screaming. No matter what I do, she is screaming. I want to hear the story; I'm hungry for stories of other people's badly behaved babies. Did Zoe find the answer? But I can't hear anything. My whole body shuts down when the baby cries. Or, that's not it—it refocuses. I can't do anything else but try to make her stop. I get on the yoga ball and bounce, bounce harder than seems okay, but it's the only thing that quiets her even a little.

"She'll be a great teenager," Louise shouts as she runs to the bathroom and returns with a wet washcloth. Between bounces, she dabs the stain on my sweater until it's gone. "All the moms with easy, sleepy babies will be checking their kids into rehab, and you'll be going to museums and doing each other's hair."

I see Taline looking at Louise in awe. Will the baby be an easy teenager? If Louise says so.

*

When I'm able to settle back onto the couch with the baby, calm and wide-eyed for the moment, Taline scoots onto the floor across the coffee table. I am about to tell her to come back—*come back!*—but then I see she moved for proximity to the pastries. She reaches over, grabs one, and finally takes a bite of a croissant Louise brought; she's been eyeing them this whole time. "Can I ask where you got her name?"

I forget, sometimes, that she even has a name. Marc and

I call her "the baby," and in my mind, that's what she is. As if there's only one in the world and she's mine.

"Marc's grandmother," I say, wiping drool with the hem of my sweater. "We're both pretty attached to her. On the flight home from Pittsburgh a few months back, I looked up from my tenth airsick baggie, and we agreed to name the baby for her."

"I didn't know you went out to see her," Taline says, glancing at Louise. I can practically see her thinking about how Louise knew about this trip while she didn't. I wasn't calling or texting Taline much these last few months—just enough so she couldn't claim that I wasn't calling or texting her. I wasn't over—maybe am still not over—how she abandoned me. It was like I was trying to prove to myself that if she didn't need to be Val and Tal anymore, I didn't either. It was that and, I guess, I didn't like to hear about it, how she got to keep being herself when suddenly I was transforming, not entirely against my will, but in a way I had little control over. Now Taline busies herself tearing apart layers of her croissant and doing everything she can, I think, to avoid looking at me. I'm not sure if I feel bad that her feelings are hurt. I bounce my knees and the baby lets out a sort of hiccupping sigh, like she's giving up and giving in to sleep, but she's not happy about it.

I start with the story, but at the sound of my voice—she *must* know it!—the baby ramps up again. Is the only solution not to speak? Can't she just give me a minute? Half of one? My eyes burning with tears I can't will away, I unzip my sweater and the baby latches as if she's famished even though she just nursed when? Like thirty seconds ago? It hurts like knives. I want to stop, but I want Taline to know the story. I want to tell her, and I need the quiet. With the baby nursing, I try to spit it all out at once. "The thing is—and thank goodness for this, of course—she's still alive. Dinah. And they're Jewish, Marc's family. You can't name a baby for someone who is still alive. The namesake is supposed to be the most recently deceased relative. We were going to take just the first letter—she was going to be Dahlia."

"Beautiful," Louise says. She has a leg folded under her, her eyes wide as she listens even though she knows this whole story already.

"So, Marc asked her," I say. "If we could do it anyway, if it would be okay with her. She said no. She basically said we'd kill her if we did that, like she'd have to die to preserve the laws of her people. But then she said what we could do was let her name the baby. I wasn't on the call. Marc was taken aback, and put on the spot, so he just agreed." The baby has her arms wrapped around my breast, the closest she gets, at this early hour, to a hug. She's still nursing even though she's now asleep, her lashes fanned out on her translucent bluish-pink cheek. Maybe the seltzer thing is a misstep and she's learned to eat while sleeping. "So, her name is Berry."

"I bet she'll love that story one day," Taline says, croissant confetti across the napkin in her lap. "But why did Dinah choose 'Berry'?" I can tell she thinks the name is strange. Which it is, I guess.

It's also strange to me that I made my peace with it so quickly. I have a small, bottom-of-my-stomach suspicion that when the hormones subside, I'll wonder what we've done. But now, for some reason, it's just a "what the hell, she's named after a fruit."

"We think it must be something dark," I say. "Because she won't elaborate."

"Or maybe she had a lover once," Taline says.

"That's exactly what Louise said," I tell her.

Louise looks up from her phone to confirm; she's probably answering a work email. Now that she runs the company, they're even more incessant. I once saw her inbox grow by 308 emails over the course of a lunch.

Taline picks a croissant flake from the napkin and places it on her tongue. "I'm sorry. I didn't know you already knew the story," she says. What would it have hurt if I'd grabbed a coffee with her and told her this story two months ago? Had she already committed arson by then?

"I think the question will come up a lot," I say, trying to be comforting. "I should get used to explaining it."

Taline smiles a smile I know isn't real, but I also know she's not trying to make me feel bad. "So, Berry it is," she says.

"She can always change it if she hates it," I say.

I am so tired, it looks like my friends are glowing, their edges gone fuzzy. It's like I can see their auras, like I *believe* in auras. Taline and Louise pick up the conversation. I hear Taline tell Louise that, in college, people called us "Val and Tal," and I feel that much more like a jerk. I can't quite follow what they're talking about after that. It's the sleeplessness, sure, but also I can't quite picture the world anymore. Is it still out there? And I am in here? This chasm is the heart of the problem. Or, one of the hearts of one of the problems.

The other heart, her head is tipped back, tiny mouth agape. I can see a bit of milk pooled in her cheek. She's so beautiful, this monster. I could cry. I do cry.

Louise shifts on the couch, leaning forward as if for a hug. "It's not real," I say. "It's hormones. I'm not sad at all." I nod, like it's decided. Louise pats my shoulder. She knows I'm lying, but she leaves it alone. Then she stands to go.

Taline asks if she should go, too. I shake my head. I don't want either of them to leave. Soon it'll be two, four, six in the morning and I'll be alone. Or, I'll feel alone. Being alone, truly alone, would be okay. It's a feeling I didn't used to appreciate. Marc will be here, sleeping when I can't because he has to work in the morning. The baby will be here; she'll always be here now. Louise bends at the waist to give me a hug. This time, I let her.

"Thank you for coming and for the snacks and the beautiful sweater, and for cleaning the beautiful sweater, and for all the coffee," I say. "I'll microwave the rest of it later and be grateful all over again."

Louise blows the baby a kiss and tells me what a good job I'm doing, as if she knows. She gives Taline a hug, too, and then eases herself out the door.

*

"I'm glad you finally met," I say. "I know you came here to meet Berry, but I'm almost more glad you met Louise."

Taline nods. "She's cool. I get it."

I'm not sure if she's being facetious or earnest. I blink as I try to figure it out and, for just a fraction of a second, fall asleep.

"Can I hold her so you can take a nap?" Taline asks.

I shake my head. "She'll wake up if I move her."

"I brought you something, too," she says. "I mean, I guess it's for her." She disappears into the hall and comes back with a small bag. I don't have the hands to open it, so Taline does it for me. She extracts a little book with Berry's name stitched on the front. Each page is a different kind of fabric embellished with simple designs and shapes. "She can chew it, spit up on it, whatever, and you can just throw it in the wash," she says. "I wanted to make a book she could read."

"It's perfect." Oh, Taline. I've missed her so much—who was I kidding? I miss her so much now. Taline sitting there right in front of me. Will it ever be the same with us again? Not because she's not here; she's here! She's right here. But where am I?

I turn the pages of the book, feeling the different textures, this one woolly, that one fluffy. I wonder if there will come a time again when I'm awake enough to read a book myself. I wonder if, after ten more weeks, I'll go back to work—my great, newish job editing literature textbooks—and be able to focus on a computer screen. Of course, I'm crying again.

"I've got to sleep," I say. I don't tell Taline to leave; I don't tell her to stay. I don't know what I want from her. I just want to close my eyes. I try to slide down into the corner of the couch so my head has a place to rest without waking the baby. I thought newborns were supposed to be able to sleep through anything, but this one, if I think the wrong thought or swallow too hard, she's up.

I'm not sure, but I get the idea I haven't been sleeping for very long when Taline wakes me. Her hand is fluttering by her face and there is a soap bubble popping, popped, on her shirt. She was doing the dishes. The baby is already awake and fussing.

I jiggle the baby, tell Taline to sit, and ask what's going on. Something is wrong. She is standing off to the side of the window, all her weight forward on her toes as she peers out through the cloak of our dingy yellow curtain.

"I was at my mother's before coming out here," she says. "In Jersey. I know how it sounds, but I think I was followed."

"By your mother?" I ask.

"Give me Berry," she says. "And just tell me what you see when you look down through those trees, where you can just see around the corner?"

I ease to my feet and pass her Berry. Standing, I have an intense urge to pee. How long have I been on that couch? Outside, the weather seems nice. "I see a cop car," I say.

"Motherfucker." Taline is in the doorway to the nursery, holding Berry, who quieted down as soon as she got settled on her shoulder. The two of them are huddled together like there's an earthquake and it's the only safe place. But should she curse like that in front of the baby?

"I don't think you were followed by the cops," I say. I lick my lips, which since I started nursing are always, always dry. "Were you?"

There are these tiny fine lines that draw down from Taline's nose to the sides of her mouth. She looks older than I remember her. "Of course not," she says. I'm not sure she's supporting the baby's head quite enough. "Not by the cops. By a cop. Just the one."

How did she get here from her mother's? She doesn't drive. "Is this about the fire?" I ask. Maybe once someone sets a fire, it's hard to stop.

"What?" She shakes her head, violently, and the baby shakes a little, too. "No, of course not."

I feel this stirring—a strange, cold slither in my arms. Taline is being followed by a police officer and she's got my baby. Another two-word term to add, finally, to the list: maternal instinct.

I hold out my arms, which feel incomplete, empty: "Can I have Berry back?"

Taline's rocking back and forth on her heels. I don't think she heard me. She launches into this story I can barely follow about breaking things off with her middle school D.A.R.E. officer.

"I told Zoe what had been going on—based on how Colin reacted, which wasn't well, it seemed like she should know. For everyone's safety. She started saying it must have been my plan all along to insinuate myself into their, like, non-affair and take him from her. In some ways, it was, but she wanted him gone! That's how it started, but then I wanted to see what it was like to sleep with a cop—this big, meaty dude we all used to crush on, you know?"

No, I shake my head. I don't know. I was feeling awful that Taline didn't know I went to see Marc's grandmother, but look what she's been keeping from me. I reach for Berry.

She leans against the doorframe, though, and continues. "There were these other times in my past when I didn't sleep with the guy I want to sleep with and then it's always this question mark. Like with Jeremiah." She pauses. "I feel like you get that."

A spark ignites. Here she is, setting a fire right here. I get the reference. Why would she bring Elliot into this? Why bring him into the same room as my baby? Taline rubs her eyes, like she's the tired one. That's what really gets me. I feel a flare, a flicker, a flame of anger. I'm the candle again and she's got the match. She's holding my baby and she's acting exhausted. What does she know? I say, "Then sometimes you go for it and drop out of school for the guy! You really run the gamut." Her eyes widen. "And if I were Zoe, I'd wonder why you picked this cop of all cops."

She switches Berry to her other shoulder, considers me. "To make him forget her," she says.

"So, that's him out there?" I ask. What kind of danger did she bring to my house today?

"The whole time, I assumed he just wanted to sleep with a former student. Zoe, me—I didn't think he cared. I'm almost positive he doesn't. But he threw a glass when I left last night. And he said *I* was threatening *him*."

My thoughts careen. I can feel every muscle in my arms twitching. "What did he mean by that?"

"Well, he didn't want me to tell Zoe. I guess he was going to try with her again?"

"Please give me Berry back," I say. My voice is sharp and louder than I thought it would be.

Taline shakes her head as if coming out of a dream and hands Berry over. My heart slows with the baby pressed against it.

"He's someone I shouldn't have gotten involved with for a lot of reasons. But none of them," she says, gathering her hair to one side of her neck and pulling it over her shoulder, "none of them make me someone who you can't trust with your baby."

"It's hard to explain. Sometimes I just need her." I try to take the edge out of my voice. "I didn't know you were involved with someone. I didn't know about the studio. You should have told me all this was going on."

"I'm not involved with him," she says. I can't stand how she's looking at me.

I turn back toward the window. The cop car is pulling out from its spot, and I see it through the clearing between the two buildings adjacent to mine.

"It's an NYPD car," I say. "And it's leaving."

She lunges for the window and presses her face against it, leaving a smudge of mascara-tears. "You're sure?"

"I'm sure," I say. I don't know what the cop cars look like where she's from, but this one, as it drives away, looks like the ones we have here.

She steps back from the window and rubs her eyes again. Mascara is everywhere. She *is* tired. Watching her, I don't know if it's the hormones or some sort of honest perspective shift, but I have the clearest, most cogent thought I've had in weeks. "What if none of it was a mistake?" I ask her.

She tilts her head and waits for me to explain. I never would have been alone in Austin if not for her, but I wanted to go to graduate school. I thought Marc was cute when I saw him across that room. And Taline wanted to sleep with a cop. To start a fire. We aren't supposed to be combustible, the two of us. This tension feels more wrong than the distance it is born from. If we are burning anything, it should be that.

"I haven't been able to shake the feeling that this isn't how things are supposed to be," I say. The baby squirms. I rub her back and she settles. "But what if this is the better timeline? What if, you know, this *is* how it's supposed to be?"

"Who knows how it's supposed to be," Taline says. "Not us, right?"

I might be a little mad forever, but in this moment, what I want is to hug her. I want to hug her, I do, but my arms are full. So she comes closer. She hugs me.

LIFEGUARDS
Cleo, 2009

WHEN HER MOTHER TELLS HER SHE IS PREGNANT, Cleo cries and cries.

"A new baby won't change the way we feel about you," her mother says.

Her father says, "Please calm down."

But Cleo won't calm down. "I thought you were *dying*."

Her mother had been looking gray and haggard, running to the bathroom at strange times, and heading up to bed hours before she usually does. There had been a series of unexplained doctor's appointments. Her mother is forty-six. What was Cleo to assume but cancer?

Her mother pulls her in for a hug, pressing her against her breasts, which are the only soft thing about her right now. She's gotten so skinny. What kind of pregnant woman gets thinner? Cleo is acting like a baby, but she is nearly sixteen and knows a thing or two. She isn't 100 percent sure she is being told the truth.

"We're just sharing with family right now," her mother says. "Only some family, actually."

Cleo wipes her eyes on her mom's ratty green pajama shirt. "But I can tell Genesis?"

Her parents exchange a look. Her father opens his mouth to answer, but her mother is quicker. She runs her hand through Cleo's hair, which is wet from the shower, tangled at the ends. "Of course," she says.

*

In the morning, while her parents are at work, Cleo and Genesis set up lawn chairs in the backyard. The Jersey summer heat is already oppressive. They open Popsicles for breakfast.

"We should have kept the wrappers on until we finished with the sunscreen," Genesis says around the Popsicle stick clenched between her teeth.

"I'll hold yours while you finish and then you hold mine," Cleo says. One in each hand, she takes small licks to keep them from dripping. Cleo had planned on telling Genesis everything right away, but now she's not sure how to start or why she feels so embarrassed. She bites off the tip of her Popsicle before handing them both to Genesis so she can slather her legs with sunscreen. Her mother purchased a strange natural kind that doesn't rub in well. It occurs to her that this, along with the uptick in organic dairy in the fridge—usually her parents go with whatever is cheapest—can be attributed to the baby. Like, is Cleo not worth the good stuff?

"Jason says he'll take us down the shore with him tomorrow," Genesis says. "And not only that." She wiggles her eyebrows. "Max is coming, too."

Jason is Genesis's big brother and Max is his BFF. He's so

totally out of the realm of possibility for either of them that it's totally fine for both of them to be totally in love with him. There's no competition. Being in love with Max is like being in love with the sun in the summertime.

"Remember last year when I got a sunburn on my back in the shape of my own hands?" Cleo asks. "I better tan even today if we're going to see Max in our freaking bathing suits."

"Stand up and spin and I'll tell you if you missed a spot," Genesis says. "This stuff is making you look like a ghost. I can see everywhere you put it."

Genesis has been Cleo's best friend for almost six years, since they were ten years old. There's no one else she'd spin in a bathing suit for.

"The area under your ponytail," Genesis says. "You missed your whole neck."

"What would I do without you?" Cleo asks, rectifying the situation. She takes a deep breath of the hot, heavy air. She spills the news. She's crying like a baby herself as she tells it.

Genesis spits out her Popsicle. She slaps her knees, shaking her head as if she has brain freeze. Maybe it's growing up with a brother; she has no patience for tears. "Is she giving birth over the summer?" she asks. "Because if we go back to school and there's a new baby suddenly, everyone is going to think it's yours."

Cleo leans back in her lawn chair so she doesn't have to look at Genesis. She gets sunblock in her eyes as she wipes them, but this fancy kind doesn't sting as much as she'd expect. She counts months on her fingers. "She's due in November. And anyway, I think everyone at school knows that I'm not having sex." Cleo is perfectly cute, but she's only just finished sophomore year and, in their school, only a few groups of sophomores are known to be having sex. The very popular kids, the drama kids, the gamers. She and Genesis are part of a nebulous crew who work on the literary journal and take the bus into the city sometimes for indie rock shows. A little quirky, maybe, but too boring for anyone to worry about.

"I guess this does answer that one question," Genesis says.

"What's that?"

"If parents still have sex," she says. "For you, the answer is yes."

*

Genesis's mom, Marianna, comes to pick her up. She pulls into the driveway and rolls down the window, extending her red-manicured hand to Cleo. She draws Cleo in for a kiss, then cups her chin, turning her face this way and that. Marianna is a dermatologist and obsessed with skincare. When patients come to the office, she takes a piece of paper with a blank outline of a person on it and marks it up with their moles, freckles, and scars. She keeps a sheet each at home for Genesis and Jason. At sleepovers, she always insists everyone wash their face. "Are you two going to do anything worthwhile this summer?" she asks. "Or just bask in the sun?"

Cleo feels another little click of understanding. Since the spring, she's been waiting for her parents to force her to enroll in a summer enrichment class or find a job as a babysitter or junior counselor or something, as they have in past years. She is old enough now to spend her days home alone, but just barely. She's never had a wide-open expanse of summer in front of her, not even when she was little. Genesis gets away with it because she spends a big chunk of the break with her grandparents in Puerto Rico; there aren't many programs she wouldn't have to cut short when she leaves. But Cleo's parents were too preoccupied this year to notice summer was coming. How will it all play out going forward? Maybe she'll be able to sneak into the liquor cabinet unnoticed, for example. But what about when she really needs them, like for help with college applications? Will they have time to proof her essays and fill out financial aid forms when there's a toddler to chase after?

"We're reading a lot," Genesis tells her mom.

"Tons. We really are," Cleo says. She and Genesis already finished two books, each reading one, then swapping to read the other. They always read the same books.

Marianna looks the two of them up and down. "Have you been smoking?" she asks.

Cleo and Genesis exchange a frown. "What?"

"You're hiding something," she says, sniffing the air, then tugging them both closer to her again. Once, the two of them did try a cigarette they swiped from Jason's floor and Marianna found them out instantly, before she was anywhere close enough to smell them. They thought she had to have been psychic. But now Cleo wonders if it was just a lucky guess. Genesis raises her eyebrows at her.

"Whatever," Cleo says. "You can tell her."

"You do it," she says. "It's not my news."

Cleo takes a breath. "My mom is pregnant," she says.

Marianna pushes her sunglasses farther up her head, even though they were there to begin with, not covering her eyes. "Wait, really?"

Cleo shrugs. "I guess."

"That's *beautiful* news," Marianna says, but Cleo can tell that she's fighting the corners of her mouth. The second she pulls out of the driveway she's going to smirk, or laugh, or say something like, "At her age?!" She had her kids two years apart like a normal person. Her job is almost done, and she did a great one. Do Cleo's parents want a do-over or something? She finds herself holding back tears again, then realizes Marianna isn't smirking like she first thought. Her eyes are full of, what, pity? Marianna squeezes her hand. "Honey, you're welcome at our house anytime."

Genesis climbs into the front seat. "We're going to pick you up really early," she says. "Jason likes to beat the traffic."

"I'll be ready," Cleo says. As they pull out of the driveway, she sits down in her backyard lawn chair again. A line of ants marches over their discarded Popsicle sticks. As she toes the warm, dry grass, she remembers seeing a video of babies being held over lawns. They'd contort in hilarious ways to keep their little bare feet from touching the grass. Babies hate grass. Babies don't sleep. They spit up, they cry, they pull hair, they are sticky. What else does she know about babies? Everyone loves them. There's this photograph on their mantle: Cleo as a newborn, curled on her father's bare, hairy chest, and her mother, long hair pulled back in a messy ponytail, bending to kiss her on the head. The way her parents' bodies are positioned literally looks like a heart curving around teeny baby Cleo. She's always loved this picture.

Through the fringe of trees at the edge of her yard, Cleo sees the yellow blur of her neighbor's dog. He's nosing around, looking for squirrels or God knows what else. Mrs. Wilson leans out her kitchen window, calling him to come back in. Her ex-husband named the dog, and now she's stuck yelling, "Dingo!" long after he moved out. Babies can be a last-ditch effort to save a marriage, she's heard. Same as on a sitcom. How many shows throw a baby in the mix to recapture their audience? Speaking of, Cleo is basically in charge of the TV when they watch as a family, picking the shows and movies they settle down in front of, with a bag of chips or a tub of ice cream. She picks the ice cream flavors. She's an only child, but she's not an asshole. Everyone thinks she's nice. She *is* nice. So what if she doesn't want to share her parents? No one told her she'd ever have to. She slips a flip-flop from her foot and slaps it down on the ants. They all survive. "Sorry, guys," she says to them. "Carry on."

*

For dinner that night, Cleo's father makes burgers on the grill, serving them with the squishy buns that Cleo likes, and the end of last summer's homemade sweet-and-sour pickles. "It's almost time to make more," he says, offering Cleo one from the tip of his fork.

"Will you have time to do it next year, I wonder?" Cleo asks.

"Maybe you can," he says. Cleo takes the pickle. It's really good, and she does love helping to make the brine and slicing the cucumbers just so. But sterilizing the jars scares her; she might give the family botulism.

"We'll make extra this summer," she says. Her parents keep staring at her, then each other, in a way Cleo finds condescending. They're probably wondering how she's taking this whole thing. Her father is drinking a cold beer, condensation gathering in an appealing manner at the bottle's rim. It is rude, she thinks, to drink when neither she nor her mother can.

Cleo sinks her teeth into her burger, watching her mother push hers around on her plate. "Mom, why are you skinnier than usual?" she asks. "That's not how it works, is it?"

"With you, no," her mother says. "With you, what happened was that I was hungrier right from the start, and only for carbs. Bagels with cream cheese, pizza crusts, stacks of white bread. I might have put a slice of white bread in between the two halves of my bagel once."

"I do like bagels," Cleo says. She feels a warmth in her, hearing about this. How silly, to be almost sixteen and feel the urge to cuddle with her mother and listen to stories about when she was in her belly.

"But, since then, the morning sickness has been brutal. The only thing that sounds good to me right now is watermelon."

Cleo's dad is guzzling his beer, which confirms for Cleo that what her mom just said was a bit off. "'Since then'?" she repeats. Her dad, as subtly as he can, is shaking his head. Her mother puts her hand over his, then takes a deep breath.

"This is the fourth time I've been pregnant since you were born," she says. "It's strange because morning sickness is often the sign of a healthy pregnancy. But, the other times, well . . . "

Cleo puts her burger down on her plate. There are tears in both of her parents' eyes. Like Cleo, they are criers, but still.

What does this mean? Genesis would make a joke. She would say, "It means your parents have been having a lot of sex." Where was I, Cleo wonders, when all of this was happening? On days when her parents had been in funny moods, or when she'd been packed off to her aunt's house for the weekend, or when her mother had forgotten to make her lunch for school, had this been the reason? She thinks back to Marianna's reaction; Marianna must have known about all of this. She knows the ways in which bodies can betray people; Cleo's mother would have entrusted her with this information even though they're just mom friends, not good friends, especially if Marianna could help keep Cleo out of her hair. Earlier, Marianna wasn't laughing or feeling bad for Cleo; she was happy.

"Miscarriages, all in the first trimester," her mother continues. "For a while, we were working with a doctor to try to get pregnant. We tried all kinds of things. Then we stopped trying, finally, and that's when I got pregnant this time. It wasn't our intention to wait until you were so much older—or until we were so much older—to have another baby. Remember, when you were small, you used to ask for a sister all the time?"

"I wanted an older sister," Cleo says. "I didn't get how it worked."

Her father laughs. "Do you still want a sister?" he asks.

"Wait, do you know?" Cleo says. "I thought you couldn't tell for a while."

"We've had a lot of tests done," her mother says. "It's a girl."

Cleo picks up her burger again. *A girl.* She gets that her parents have wanted this baby for a long time. But, at this point, she doesn't get why they still want it. Like, what if the universe was telling them that they had everything they needed?

"What if there's something wrong with the baby?" Cleo says. "Like, what if it wasn't working for a reason?"

Her mother leans back in her chair at the same time as her father leans forward. "What a thing to say," he says.

Cleo narrows her eyes at him. "Why did you make burgers when all Mom wants is fruit?"

"You like burgers," he says.

"It isn't about me," Cleo says. *A girl.* "Not anymore." She takes her mother's burger from her plate and leaves the table.

From her room, she can hear her parents talking, the low murmur of their voices rising through the heating grate in her floor, but not what they are saying. Eventually, one of them comes to knock on her door. She doesn't answer, and when whomever it is cracks it—her father, she thinks—she pretends to be sleeping, even though it is only 9:00 and the lights are still on. He goes away, which, as she sniffles into her pillow, she understands isn't actually what she wanted. If she's going to be replaced, it hasn't happened, or shouldn't happen, quite yet.

*

Genesis calls to run through her bathing suit options with Cleo, who answers in a whisper from under the covers, keeping up the ruse that she's asleep. They know each other's wardrobes down to the sock, so when Genesis asks if she should wear the one with the cherries or the tangerine-colored triangle, Cleo knows exactly what she's talking about. "Save the orange for when you're a little tanner," she says. "The white with the cherries will look good now."

"You aren't going to wear a one-piece, are you?" Genesis asks.

"Yeah," Cleo says. "You know how I feel about bikinis."

Cleo loves the beach but wishes it didn't have to involve bathing suits. It's not even about body issues, or it's mostly not. She looks fine. It's the comfort of it. Something is always riding up, slipping down, or tugging to the side. Sand gets in under the elastic. She likes when her clothes are simple and comfortable enough to fade into the background so she doesn't have to think about them on top of everything else she thinks about. A bathing suit is always in the foreground, causing trouble.

"But Max," Genesis says, whining.

"Why would you complain about looking better than me?" Cleo asks. She's happy that they're going to the beach with Jason and Max because she loves the waves, and it's fun to whisper about Max and look at his dreamy eyes, but she harbors no illusions he'd ever be interested in her, or really in Genesis either. He's a veritable celebrity who happens to be friends with Genesis's brother. They're in the same place as him all the time and he never pays them any attention. True, it isn't usually just the four of them, but on the off chance he happens to glance at her, is it worth looking just a tiny bit cuter versus having to worry about losing her top while diving under a wave?

"Honestly, two-pieces are more comfortable. They pull less. You can move better."

Cleo considers this. "Really?"

"Swear to God," Genesis says. "How about you wear the orange one?"

"I'll wear the cherries," Cleo says. "But I'm bringing my Speedo in case you're lying."

*

In the morning, they're in their bikinis, jean shorts, and flip-flops, crammed into the backseat of Jason's car along with everyone's towels, a cooler with fruit and sodas, sunblock, Frisbees, and a set of speakers.

Cleo gestures to the speakers. "I hate when people play music at the beach," she whispers to Genesis. "Half the reason to go there is to listen to the ocean."

Max turns around, his wild brown hair whipping in the wind rushing through the open windows. Cleo doesn't know how he heard her. He says something about how he has someone's new album—she has no idea who he's talking about—and that it feels more like a party with music. Cleo smiles at him but rolls her eyes at Genesis. A second after she does it, she realizes that Jason is looking at her in the mirror; he rolls his eyes right back.

Once they've arrived, found parking, and set up on the sand, Genesis pulls out a tube of sunblock and they start to apply. She says, "Jason, you better put it on, too. Can you imagine what Mom would say if you came home with a sunburn?" He groans but begins to smear lotion all over his legs and arms.

Max strips off his shirt and fiddles with the music, drinking a soda. Cleo and Genesis exchange looks.

"You need some, too," Genesis says. "You're real pale."

"All the more reason to get a tan," he says. He doesn't wink, but the way he says it implies a wink.

"Believe me," Cleo says. "She isn't going to let this go until you put on the sunblock."

He pauses, then grabs the tube from Jason. "Get my back?" he says to Cleo. "And I'll get yours?".

"Ask Jason," she says. "And I'll ask Genesis." She won't be flirted with just to be strung along, but as she watches him contort to rub lotion onto his own back, she thinks maybe she was too quick to answer; maybe it would have been nice to feel his smooth, sharp shoulder blades and the two little divots above the waistband of his suit. Why do boys, the cutest boys, have those dimples there?

Genesis swipes the lotion from him and skims it over his back. She raises her eyebrow at Cleo like, *Is this so hard?* As Cleo watches, it's clear why Max asked her and not his friend's sister: Jason glares at him as Genesis makes sure he's fully lubed up. As soon as she's done, Max says, "Okay, let's go in!" but Genesis wants to wait a few minutes. So instead they spread out their towels, and Max fires up that new album he was talking about, something poppy and more fun than Cleo had imagined. They all smell good, the sun is out, and it isn't too hot. The bikini doesn't ride up in the same way a one-piece does; Genesis wasn't lying about that.

"Can we do this every week?" Cleo asks.

"Every day?" Genesis echoes.

"Yeah," Jason says. "Until we leave for . . .

"Shhh," Cleo says, not wanting a reminder that, for the second half of the summer, she'll be on her own. Sure, she has other friends, but it's not the same.

On a blanket next to them, Cleo hears a woman grumbling about how loud their music is. Cleo opens one eye and takes her in. She's got on a black one-piece suit, the kind that is gathered in the middle to hide a tummy, and her hair is tied back with a batik scarf. She's holding a bucket for a small, sturdy toddler who is tossing in handfuls of wet sand as she babbles, too little to talk yet. The bucket looks heavy, and the mother looks like she's not enjoying herself, like she wasn't even before Cleo and her friends sat down with their music. The little girl misses the bucket and the sand lands on her mother's thigh. "Berry, you're killing me," she says with a deep sigh.

There's a pair of large men's sandals on the blanket, but the man is nowhere to be seen. Here's one kind of future, Cleo thinks. My parents will be stressed out by the new baby, whether she replaces me or not. They'll stop having fun together, with me, or by themselves. The baby will ruin life not only for me but for everyone. She pokes her own stomach, which has some give to it, and imagines it taut and round. What would it be like to get kicked from the inside? It would be perfectly normal timing for her to have a baby in ten years or so. By then, her parents' new baby will still be in elementary school. Why would they get excited to have a grandkid when their own child still wants to sit on their laps?

She scans the beach for other ways to be. There are plenty of young, beautiful people, their bikini tops untied as they lie facedown on the sand, or holding their hands up to shield their eyes from the sun as they flirt with each other, ankle-deep in the surf. "Let's go in the water," she says.

The four of them make their way to the ocean's edge, leaving their bags and the radio in that trusting way people do when they're down the shore. The water is a lot rougher than

Cleo had realized before they got up close. The waves are coming at them fast and churning, the sound of them a roar, and the smell of them sharp and saline. "This is scary!" Genesis shouts, losing her footing a bit. Her arms shoot out to the sides for balance. Cleo grabs one and Max the other. Jason takes Cleo's free hand and they continue on in chain formation. The water is so painfully cold that they are all hopping up and down, shrieking. Jason squeezes her hand and smiles at her with this happy, childlike abandon, and she thinks, *Oh*. She thinks, *Jason*. Maybe, when circumstances change, they don't always change for the worse.

Down the beach a little, the mother, her toddler, and a man in a long-sleeved rash guard, who must be the father, are also wading in. Cleo looks away from them, focusing on her friends instead.

They're thigh-deep now and jumping up as each wave crests, their heads just above the surface. It's too hard for them all to stay connected so Cleo and Genesis let go of each other, trailing their fingers off with a little tickle to the palm. Max lifts Genesis up and tosses her into the water. Even though she never wants to get her hair wet—not after spending so long getting those baby hairs just so—she laughs. Cleo's watching them, wondering if something actually might happen, when she realizes Jason has been talking to her. She turns to him and he says, pointing ahead, "I think we need to go under this one!"

The wave is enormous, the kind surfers are atop when their pictures get taken. Behind them, people are running for the shore. "Scared?" she asks Jason, teasing. She lets go of his hand to hold her nose and when the wave's almost on top of her, she dives.

Down, down, the water is cold, streaming through her hair, the murk of the sand kicked up and swirling around her, the violent roil tearing at the strings of her bikini top and pulling at the bottom. She reaches to hold the pieces so they don't rip off from her body. Wishing for her Speedo, she gets caught up in the current, flips, hits her shoulder with a scrape, a bump, her lungs get hot, she kicks, kicks, pushes off the silty floor of the sea, emerges into the summer air with a burst. Bathing suit askew but intact. A body knocks against her legs, hard, nearly sending her back down into the surf. She feels a sharp bite, a cling—shark?!—but then she feels fingernails and she thinks, Jason, what a wimp, she reaches down and it's the baby. Cleo lunges for the tiny body, hard to do with the little arms wrapped so tight around her legs. She wrenches her free and pulls her up to the surface. The baby's quiet and squirming, then with a rush comes water, screams. Now her nails are digging into Cleo's back as the baby holds on for her life. She's cold and smooth and vibrating with fear. "I've got you," Cleo says, gasping, her breath not quite caught. "I've got you."

It's not just the baby screaming but everyone, it seems. First Jason is there, anchoring Cleo as she makes her way to the shore, then the father in the rash guard. He's making it worse, trying to get the baby away from Cleo and into his arms when there are waves still coming and Cleo is the better swimmer. An instant later, there are the lifeguards. They pull the father back and take the baby. Cleo knows to let go, to let the professionals help now, but relieved of that little body, she shakes. Another lifeguard helps her and Jason to shore.

At the surf's edge, Genesis and Max, who must not have been out far enough to get sucked into the wave, run for Cleo and Jason, grabbing their hands and towing them toward the gathered crowd. The mother in the black bathing suit is hyperventilating on the sand next to where the lifeguards are huddled around the baby, swatting away anyone who tries to pat her back. The father is leaning so far over the group that it looks like he might fall and flatten them all. It's scary, even though Cleo knows for a fact that the baby is not dead. She can still feel bright spots on her shoulder blades and her leg where those little fingernails dug in. What else do babies know, really, other than how to survive?

Finally, the lifeguards let the mother at her daughter. She swoops down and scoops her into her arms, the father joins, and they all fold together, tight, one unit. The lifeguards, young, mostly men, disperse, relieved and laughing. One of them gives Cleo a high five as he heads back to his chair.

"You saved that kid," Genesis says, both arms around her. She feels warm and dry against Cleo's clammy skin. "I feel like they should thank you? Like, for doing their job?"

Jason says, "Maybe they'd get in trouble for not having been the ones, you know? We were out there for a minute before anyone else came to help."

"We," Max teases, slapping Jason on the back. "That was all your girl there, not you."

Cleo scratches her head, her hair stiff with salt and sand. "I'll be right back," she says.

She wiggles out of Genesis's grasp, dizzy from her tumble as she makes her way over beach towels to the family. The mother is sitting on their blanket, cradling the little girl, who is curled against her chest, sucking her thumb, as the father shoves all their things into a big bag. She crouches down at the edge of the blanket.

The mother's face is pale, a worry line tight on her brow. "Are you hurt?"

"Me?" Cleo says. "I'm fine. How is she?"

The woman kisses her daughter, lips pressing hard on her matted hair. "You must think I'm a terrible mother."

This is the last thing Cleo expected her to say. She shakes her head. "Of course not."

"I was holding her, and the wave came. I don't know how I could have let go."

"It was really strong," Cleo says. "It pulled my bathing suit off."

"It's just . . . shouldn't my instincts have been better?" She cups her daughter's head in her hand, running her thumb along the baby's cheek.

Why would anyone choose this? This terrible responsibility, this worry, this guilt.

"I'm glad she's okay," Cleo says. When she turns around, the boys are playing with a Frisbee, but Genesis is back on her towel. The music is off. Cleo pads across the sand to take her place beside her friend, lying on her stomach, watching the family until they're fully packed up to go. They leave without saying goodbye.

Genesis says, "This is a story they'll tell forever. The time they almost lost their baby at the beach."

Cleo saw it in that mother, this desperate desire to hang on, this desperate inability to hang on. Her parents chose to do it with her, and they chose it again, and again, and again, and again.

"We'll tell the story, too," Cleo says. "Until we have a better one."

THIRTY-TWO
Val, 2010

WHEN BERRY REFUSES TO UNCLENCH the bunched-up fabric of my skirt, when she refuses to join the rest of the kids in her ballet class inside the studio, when she refuses to say what the problem is, I basically lose it.

I mean, I don't. Not really. But I hiss, "You love this class. Please go. Just get over there."

She stands frozen, her face impassive. I give her a little shove. Nothing. "You're a Not Scary Ghost!" I say. Her small curly head pokes out of a hole I cut in a white crib sheet. I used iron-on letters to spell out NOT SCARY GHOST, per her request. It's adorable. I try again. "You have to go show the other kids your costume. It's almost Halloween! It's your special Halloween class! Look, Mario is dressed as a puppy! Look, Eliana is Elmo! Go."

She lifts a corner of her costume, sticking the sheet into her mouth and chewing. So then I say, "Do we have to leave?" I turn around and walk toward the door. Usually this does the trick. Usually, she doesn't really want to go. But today I guess she does because she walks calmly toward the door right along with me. No digging in her heels. I hate myself for the tactical misstep. I give her one more chance to go in. Nothing. I have no choice; I have to follow through. That's what the people on the internet say. She has to start learning to understand consequences. I grab her by the arm and tug her into the hall. Now she's crying. She was coming willingly; there was no reason for the tug. Behind me, fifteen caregivers avert their eyes.

I'm so mad I feel it in my temples. But, like Berry, I can't quite articulate why. What is the problem with leaving dance class, exactly? I mean, there's the money. The teacher is worth it, but it's a feat of budgeting to make it work. As we skulk toward the stairs, I hear her guiding the tiny children through a series of moves, using the actual ballet words: plié, plié, échappé! We tried a dance class before this one where the teacher was all "pizza feet" and "diamond legs" and Berry, a purist, was appalled. I was fine échappéing that one.

On the street, I look up at the holding-pen window, sure that there will be a row of parents and nannies watching to see if I'm still viciously pulling Berry like an absolute monster now that we're outside. What a poorly behaved mother, they're thinking. I don't see anyone, but that doesn't mean they're not there.

On the ten-block walk home, I rake my hand through my unbrushed hair, knowing it looks ridiculous. I can feel how red in the face I am. I used to think this bedraggled look was a costume—new-mom drag—and I'd cast it off, getting back to normal soon enough. Now I wish I had a sheet over my head like Berry, except also covering my face. Like those moms in the old photographs Taline showed me once, sitting under blankets to prop up their kids for a studio portrait. A faceless piece of furniture.

We round the corner, almost to our place, and there at a charmingly off-kilter table at our local café sit two women, drinking their lattes, deep in conversation. I can't keep the longing off my face. The forty-five minutes while Berry is in dance class and I'm on the other side of the door, sitting alongside the other adults on a narrow wooden bench—the kids are two and three, so we're supposed to stay on the premises in the event of potty needs or meltdowns or nosebleeds—those forty-five minutes are the only guaranteed time during the week that I get to talk to other grown-ups. I work from home: during the two precious half days of daycare a week, and then before she wakes up, after she goes to bed, from tree stumps on the playground, and through copious amounts of screentime. I'm either with Berry or I'm at my computer. It's not really by choice; it's financial necessity. Or financial privilege, or some combination of the two. In any case, I used to have coffee with friends. Now I have forty-five minutes of dance class to talk to some people with whom most of what we have in common is kids the same age. But guess what? That's enough!

*

I say all of this to Berry, who is two and three-quarters years old.

*

We never go to this café ourselves because it's too close to our apartment. I know if we do it once, we'll never be able to pass it by without a meltdown again. I tell Berry that if you go there, they make you drink coffee, so each time we pass, she shouts, *Coffee is NOT for kids!* The last time I had an existential crisis in front of it was a mere two weeks ago. We were elbows deep in potty training. When Berry has to go, she has to go, and what a victory it is if she tells me with enough notice that I can whip out the travel potty, preloaded with a plastic bag. She said, "Mama, time to pee!" And, thrilled—even though, yes, we'd just left the house and she could have used the actual toilet there—I set up her commode on the sidewalk just behind a tree and then, when she was done, I helped her wipe and gave her a high five. Then I realized that while she was behind a tree regarding the cars on the street, she was right in front of the café and this group of twentysomething guys was sitting there, noses scrunched. They were the kind of guys who, ten years ago—no, five years ago—might have bought me a beer, might have actively tried to get me to go home with them at the end of a night out. Now they have no reason to notice me, generally, except when I do things like have my kid pee right out in the open, a slim shield of glass between the bag of urine in my hand and their egg sandwiches. I wanted to think that, one day, they'll be where I was, too, but of course they won't be. They'll be at work.

We get to our building, haul up three flights, and stagger through the door—literally stagger because Berry is clinging to my leg, impeding both of our movements and making me long for a time when I could go a few hours without being touched by another person. I turn on the TV because, although I don't want to reward Berry with TV—TV is still, somehow, a reward—I need a moment to regroup. Before I change the channel, I see a flash of a news story about the midterms, some clown raving about private insurance. I click away and thankfully Berry's favorite show, the one with the enervating singing baby, is on.

Within five minutes she's asleep on the couch. I wish I'd taken her costume off, so it wouldn't be wrinkled for actual Halloween on Sunday. It's been wonderful, the last two years, enjoying Halloween again. Berry's been the perfect avatar, an all-consuming vessel I could dress up—as a plump pierogi her first year and a Cabbage Patch doll, complete with signature on the tush, her second—and revel in, without having to think about Halloweens past, or myself, at all. I used to deflect from my birthday with my own costume, but a cute baby in a costume—that really did the trick. No one remembered I even existed. It looks like, this year, it won't be that simple. One thing goes wrong and I'm spiraling. Since having Berry, I can't stop projecting forward from each mistake I make, seeing how it will compound each moment after, making everything worse. Ten years after that Halloween with Elliot—is it eleven years?—I don't feel that same level of dread about Halloween, not the way I used to, but it is there in the background, coloring my anxiety a little darker. It all still gets to me, and I'm probably taking it out on Berry, like a terrible, terrible mother.

Watching Berry sleep, sprawled on her back and sucking her thumb, I remember how many times she showed up in our doorway last night. She's not going to bed earlier like she's supposed to even though she dropped her nap, despite my best efforts to cling to it. She was too tired for dance class. And too little to know it, unlike me.

I text Taline: *I can't decide if I want to be my own person or obliterate that person forever.*

What? she responds. *Say more?!*

I tell her what happened and how I behaved. I tell her that Halloween has started early this year. I tell her that I don't know what to do with myself.

You're doing your best!

I am not sure if this is true, but if it is, that doesn't seem good. I curl up on the opposite side of the couch, across from Berry, and bury my head in my arms. Maybe if I rest, too. But it's like my bones want to climb out of my skin. How would that be for a Halloween costume?

No—this can't be my best. I try to match my breathing to Berry's little snores. In and out. I press my feet against hers and Berry presses back: a small, sleepy pas de deux. We stay like that, toe to toe, until I have to wake her up. I don't want to, but we'll pay at bedtime if she sleeps any longer. I crouch beside her and rub her back until she opens her eyes.

"Did you know my birthday is soon?" I ask her. "It's on Halloween."

She sits with the information for a second before putting her face so close to mine that our noses touch. Hers is cold, wet as always. She clamps a small sticky hand on to each of my cheeks. "Let's bake a cake," she says.

I almost say no. Soon is not now. A cake baked now won't last until soon. But I don't say no. I push the noes out of my mind. I say, "Let's go to the kitchen and see what we find."

SATURDAY, NEW YORK CITY
Taline, 2010

"THE OTHER DAY, ON THE TRAIN, there was a woman with this unreal, hacking cough. Which, fine, it happens, but she wasn't covering her mouth or anything. Flagrantly spewing germs. And giving dirty looks to anyone who looked at her or edged away from her, like we were the ones being public health hazards! Everyone crowded over to the other side of the car, waiting until the doors opened so we could get out. Everyone, that is, except the man she was with. She was with a man!"

We are walking down Central Park West, clutching our coffees to keep their heat close in this late-autumn cool. Val smacks me, hard, on the arm. "You're a disgrace," she says. "An absolute disgrace."

"You already guessed the moral of the story, then?" I ask, taking a pull of coffee.

"Don't say it," she says. "Don't you dare."

"If *she* can find a man . . . "

She holds out her hand. "I need your card," she says. "I'm revoking your membership to feminism."

I give her my hand and we walk like that, into the park.

*

We find a looming gray rock formation on which to perch. Reaching into our bags, we extract gigantic egg sandwiches and dig in, balancing the dregs of our coffees on the natural ledge between us. Mouth full, she humors me.

"You don't know what it's like," I tell her. "These dating sites go out of fashion so fast. For ten minutes, I'm on the right one, with the interesting, employed men, and then all of a sudden they've moved on and it's only polyamorous barbacks, art handlers, and bass players left."

"Didn't Louise tell you about one she thought was good?" she asks.

She tries to keep her face normal, but I can tell by the way her mouth twitches that she still doesn't love Louise and me hanging out. When we are all together, that's one thing. What she doesn't love is that we are friends now even without her involvement. That we text and go to happy hour. It's not that we don't invite her—we always do—but what are the chances she can get away from bath time or bedtime or whatever other time to come meet us? Louise and I, we have time. And yeah, she did tell me about the dating site she thought was good.

"I'm telling you," I say. "Bass players and barbacks!"

"That seems judgmental," Val says. "I mean, you're an artist! And it's not like, traditionally, you've had a hard time finding men to fall in love with you, right?"

"Are you kidding?" My throat tightens as I think about the

list of jokers she must be referencing. "Some of those people, their interest in me was practically criminal."

"Well, I'd take my time if I were you," she says. "And don't forget about cocktail parties, bookstores. You know, real life."

"You're the only person I know who settled down with someone they met in real life," I say.

She practically flinches.

"What?" I ask. "You don't like me saying that you're 'settled'? I only mean that in the best way. You know how I feel about Marc."

"How *do* you feel about Marc?" she asks. She is sly, like she wants me to convince her.

"Did I see that he got *wire-rimmed* glasses? As if he needed anything else to complete the picture," I say. "The world's most crushable English teacher." I'm always a little anxious that she'll leave him. It's like he's so good for her that she can't see it. Without any friction, he disappears to her. "I mean, I don't want to get all gross about your husband—you know. You do. Meanwhile, I'm like a founding member of half the dating sites out there. I've been doing this since before phones were good enough to send dick pics. That's all I mean. It's exhausting."

"I was on there with you in the beginning, too, remember?" she says. "I'd always stall out at the messaging phase, though. There'd be too much writing back-and-forth and I'd realize I probably hated the dude before we even met. I'll have no dick pic stories to share with Berry when she's older."

"Thank goodness for that," I say. "Anyway, nice day, huh? It reminds me of college. Fall was always so great there.

Remember when we lived together, that tree outside the window? It practically glowed in the fall, so red and lit up and autumnal."

Val nods. "What's especially nice is walking through the park at an adult pace, admiring the leaves but not bending to pick up each one and not having to save the crumbliest and brownest in my pockets. Not that I don't love experiencing the world through Berry's eyes, but toddler-vision can really slow a person down. This—this feels great. No one is touching me. No one is tugging at me. I have a coffee that is almost finished and yet is still hot, and no one who is not allowed to drink it has begged for a sip."

"You really paint a picture," I say.

Her attention drifts down the path in front of us and she starts waving. "I think I went to high school with her," she says.

I can't believe it. I'd know her anywhere: the lithe frame, glossy hair, and poreless skin all aglow beneath a luxurious camel hair coat and giant tortoiseshell sunglasses. I swat Val's hand out of the air. "That's a *movie star*," I say. "You don't know her."

"Really? She looks so familiar."

"In the nineties, she had a haircut named after her," I say. "She's so successful that she only does films she *believes in* now. Your high school did not produce anyone who looks like that."

"Oh yeah," she says. "Didn't we go see her in something at that two-dollar theater in college? I think that's the last thing I saw her in."

I shake my head. "You're really out of the loop, huh." I mean it to be a fond comment, but even I hear that it doesn't quite come across that way.

Val draws her jacket tighter around her shoulders, watching for a moment. Then she says, "Goddamn is she beautiful."

We slide off the rock, crumpling our sandwich wrappers into our emptied coffee cups, and, without exchanging another word, begin to follow her.

*

The Movie Star is on her own. She's not drinking or eating anything, nor is she on the phone or listening to music. It's noteworthy, in this day and age, when a person seems to be out simply enjoying the day.

"It's just anthropological curiosity," Val says. "That's all this is."

"I'd like some shoes like that," I say. The shoes are phenomenal: black clogs with wooden heels, but somehow better than that. Val points down at her own feet. She's got on similar shoes, a fact I didn't notice until just now. They're not quite as good as the Movie Star's but almost. Maybe as an artifact of her fashion days, Val still knows how to score a great pair of shoes. I start to ask her where she got them, but she shushes me. She's focused on the Movie Star.

We wind, the three of us, through the park's walkways, littered with orange and yellow leaves, until we get to the reservoir. Following just a few feet behind her—too far and it would seem like we are stalkers when, of course, we have nothing to hide— we mount the stairs that lead up to the pebbly circular path and start around, headed east. The Movie Star's pace is leisurely, far slower than we're used to walking. We could lap her if we wanted. We watch the sinewy way she moves and how she adjusts her big purple purse when it starts to slide down: she lifts it with a quick bump of her hip, then settles it back on her shoulder. The purse is the perfect punctuation to her otherwise understated outfit. She's probably ten years older than us and yet there's nothing middle-aged about her, except maybe her confidence.

"Not to be my own counterpoint," I whisper. "But *she* is single."

"And childless?" Val asks. "Those hips haven't birthed a human being, that's for sure. I guess you can have kids, or you can look like that."

I hold out my hand. "Give me back my card or I'm taking yours."

"Point taken. Don't tell Berry I said that."

"Berry's a toddler," I say. "I don't gossip with her on the regular."

"She's old enough," Val says. "The other day she called cookies a guilty pleasure. It took me twenty minutes to decipher what she was saying. You know, her *L*s all still sound like *W*s. I traced the sentiment back to one of the other moms from the playground."

"I can't imagine what it would be like to have a daughter whose relationship to food you have to worry about," I say. "To *shape*. My mother didn't do a great job with that."

"It *is* a job," Val says. "But Cookie Mom is a bad colleague. I've been realizing that I need to make a better effort to see you, Louise—my actual adult friends—more often."

"You deserve it!" I say.

She shakes her head. "I don't know if *deserve* is the right word. I've just been having these moments lately I'm not proud of. Even though I'm actively trying to work on my patience. On being present. Like the other day, Berry took off her shoes at the playground. When I told her to put them back on, she picked them up and threw them, like really hard. One of them hit this other kid in the face. I just stood there wishing I was at work. At a real job."

"Editing is a real job," I say.

Val shakes her head. "Anyway, a day or so later, I realized that Berry had outgrown the shoes. They were hurting her, and she actually *had* told me that before we left the house, but I was like, You always wear them and they're always fine, so you're wearing them today. But that's what happens with kids and shoes—one day they fit and the next they don't. I should know that. I have one job, you know?"

I wait to see if she registers what is so obvious to me, but she doesn't seem to, so I say, "You've been telling me for the past ten minutes about how that is literally not the case."

She gives me the same pensive look that I've been giving her. Then she says, "I can see you as a stay-at-home mom. You'd have all the crafts and snacks and sing-alongs and nap schedules down to a tee."

I like this assessment. Lately, I've been thinking this same thing. When I was younger, I always worried I'd have to choose at some point: art or family? That's what the Movie Star did— the will-she or won't-she of motherhood was always in the tabloids. Did she have a baby bump or just eat a sandwich that day? She chose art, or so it seems from the outside anyway. It wasn't so much the options that made me anxious but the prospect of making the choice. But, unlike the Movie Star, maybe it was never up to me. I was evicted from my studio; no one got my work. I didn't make a choice so much as an option was eliminated. Not that I have a viable path to motherhood right now either. "Should I put that in my dating profile?" I ask. "Willing to quit working to take care of babies?"

"Speaking of working," Val says, gesturing ahead at the Movie Star, "do you think she feels about her job the way we do about ours?"

I shake my head. "No way," I say, shielding my eyes to watch her. "She's got real power."

"Have you heard back from that museum?" Val asks. "The interview you told me about?"

"I just had a teaching audition in the galleries," I say, kicking some leaves from our path. "If I get it, I think I can quit two of my other jobs. It went sort of great. Like, way better than any of my dates have gone lately. But I haven't heard yet. And, as always, it's contractual work—no healthcare, no benefits. A bit of cachet and better pay, though."

"Will it leave you time to paint?" she asks, kicking leaves, too. "If you get it?"

People fall into two camps when they hear that I'm not painting anymore: those who wish I would and those who are relieved I'm not. "I'm more interested in other people's art right now," I say. "Actually, I just saw this artwork that made me think of you and Berry."

"Oh yeah?"

"It's this series of short video pieces by Lenka Clayton. She set up a camera in different locations, like a grocery store or a big field, and filmed her baby toddling off into the distance.

You watch as he gets farther and farther away. When his mother, the artist, can't take it anymore, she bursts into the frame, tearing after him. It's as if they're connected by a thread and just when it's about to snap, she runs, relieving the tension. A number, the distance he managed to put between them, flashes on the screen and that's the end. So simple and so smart. Really moving. Kinda funny."

"I lost her in the grocery store the other day," Val says, biting her lip. "And want to know the worst part? I didn't notice. I got to the bulk goods section, and she was already there, a store worker crouched down next to her, trying to figure out her name. She spotted me and started yelling, 'Mama, Mama,' and I had to pretend I'd been looking for her. Really, I'd been looking for the black beans. I was so focused on what to feed her for dinner that I forgot about . . . her."

Lost in conversation, we almost lose the Movie Star. She's veered off the path. I feel a flicker of disappointment, but Val, she's craning her neck, looking all over. We regain sight of her as she rounds the playground behind the Met, its pyramids teeming with screaming children, and catch up to her before she exits onto Fifth Avenue.

"The east side," I say. "Whoops." We're meeting Marc and Berry back across the park at the Natural History Museum.

"We've got an hour," Val says. "Let's let this play out. We haven't learned any of her secrets yet. What do you think the moral of the story is going to be?"

"Stars," I say. "They're just like us. Or maybe, stars: they're so different from us that we shouldn't feel bad about our failures."

Now that we're on the street, other people begin to recognize the Movie Star. Heads turn. If it were another part of town, a part populated by actual New Yorkers, no one would approach her, but we're in tourist territory. The social mores are different. We hang back along the low stone fence that flanks the park while she engages in a group photo op.

"What's your prediction?" I ask Val. "Where's she going next?"

"A magazine shoot? A dress fitting? The apartment of a very rich and handsome man?"

I shake my head. "Can you imagine how much maintenance she's got to do? Maybe she's going for highlights or Botox."

Val puts an index finger to the double lines between her eyebrows. I'd never noticed them before. "Maybe she'll take us with her," she says. *Us?* Do I have those lines, too? I reach up to check. Not yet. So far, it's just the ones beside my mouth.

When the Movie Star pauses, we do, too, leaning against the fence and watching her from half a block away. We can't take our eyes off of her. She is both reserved and somehow radiant as she greets her public. "Gosh, she's swarmed," I say.

The Movie Star takes a step back to place her bag on the wall. When she turns to wrap her arms around some teenaged girls, I can smell the jasmine scent of her hair as she tosses it over her shoulder. That's when I realize how much closer we've inched. The girls are shrieking as they attempt a selfie, leaning this way and that to try to fit everyone in the frame. I tilt my head, gesturing us along with my jaw. *We need to give it up*, I try to telegraph to Val. We're no better than these tourists and kids if we just sit here waiting to see where she's going next. I slide off the wall and continue down the street, walking with purpose past the Movie Star, pretending my hardest not only that we haven't been following her, but that I haven't noticed her at all.

At the corner, I glance over at Val. It takes me a moment to make sense of what I'm seeing. Even when I think I know what I'm looking at, it defies understanding.

Val's got the Movie Star's bag, the big purple elephant of it, clutched to her chest. "Smell this leather," she says.

I tear my eyes from Val and look back down the street— the Movie Star is still taking pictures. She doesn't know yet. If I grab it from Val, could I return it before the Movie Star notices?

"You won't believe this," I hear her say. "It felt light when I picked it up and it's because, look! It's *empty!*"

I lean over, ever so slightly, to confirm. The inside of the bag is silk, monogrammed, and yes, totally empty. Maybe she is on her way to pick something up. Maybe she just likes the way it completes her outfit. I hear rumblings behind us. I can't look back again, but my guess is that the theft—that's what this is, right, a theft?—has been noticed. I make eye contact with Val. "*Run,*" I say.

We're not big on exercise, we two. We make it running only a block and a half, then we're barely jogging, panting. Val is laughing. On some level, she must know she's lost her mind, but that level isn't the one in charge right now. All I can think is that I have to help her undo this. Speed walking, we make brisk progress up Fifth Avenue. On our right is the Guggenheim Museum. There's a line out the door to the main entrance, but there's a side door that goes straight into the gift shop. I shove Val toward it.

"What are you doing?" she asks, dipping her head to sniff the bag.

"We're going to ditch it," I say. "In there." I push Val into the revolving door and follow her, squishing into one slot. As we rotate, I see her—the Movie Star—hurrying up the block. I think she's coming right for us.

Once inside, we jag left to the museum shop. It's jammed with tourists. I pull Val behind me as we weave around them, and when we're in the middle, between the umbrellas and the Frank Lloyd Wright scarves, I snatch the bag—she's reluctant, still, to give it up, fingertips trailing it as I pull it from her— and toss it, underhand, to the side. It makes a dull *oof* as it hits a display bin. My eyes go to the ceiling, to the corners of the room—there must be security cameras everywhere. Thank goodness this isn't the museum where I just interviewed. It would have been so much easier to toss the bag while we were still outside. We could have chucked it and kept moving. I am an awful criminal.

The Movie Star is just entering the shop as we're looping back toward the door. We stare each other down across a bin of snow globes. I see our own wild faces twinned in the Movie Star's tortoiseshell glasses.

"Hey!" she shouts. The entire shop stops to stare. The Movie Star is international. Folks drop their goods and move toward her. She is consumed by the crowd. I keep hold of Val's arm, and we skirt her, slipping out the door into a taxi stopped at the light on the corner.

*

In the cab crosstown, I stare at Val. I take her in. Her face is flushed but not, I don't think, from embarrassment. She seems exhilarated. She seems, I think, happier than I've seen her in a long time. "That was a real exercise in privilege," I tell her. "Not just anyone could steal a bag like that and get away with it."

"I didn't think about that," she says.

"Right."

She covers her face with her hand. "Point taken," she says. "I didn't mean to steal it. I just—I had to know what it felt like to have it."

"And?" I ask. "What did it feel like?"

"Amazing," she says. "I'm sorry, but it did."

*

Marc and Berry are in front of the Museum of Natural History, looking wind-chapped and pleased with themselves. "No underwear," Berry announces, pulling down her rainbow leggings to reveal a diaper. Val is aghast, glaring at her husband.

He leans in and I hear him whisper, "She *told* me she was going to pee her pants. It was a foregone conclusion. Better safe than sorry, right?"

I try to stifle my laughter as Val shakes her head and gives him a shove. "You won't be the one stuck at home for another whole week now," she says. "Restarting the whole process." Val hugs her arms to her body. It's like she's conjuring back the bag, like she's clutching its phantom presence to her chest.

I wonder if, later, I should shoot Marc a text, let him know what happened, and ask him to keep an eye on her. I try to initiate meaningful eye contact with him. What is he thinking? Is he worried? He doesn't look worried. Does he know better than I do? I do catch his eye. He looks wearier than he used to, a bit more weatherworn and tired. Somehow, it works for him; he's one of those men who will only get better and better looking. "You haven't met my buddy Mitchell yet, have you?" he asks me.

"I've met so many people's buddies," I say. "Maybe not yours, though." If Marc knows what I want, he must have a handle on what his own wife does. Right?

"I'll give him your number?" he asks. I blush and nod. How can I like him, this Mitchell, already? I hear the name, the mere mention of some prospective partner, and fill in the rest. I project a future.

"Go to the gym," Val says to him. He goes to hand her the diaper bag and, as she reaches for it, I leap to intercept it. I hoist it onto my shoulder instead. Somehow, I think if she got it in her hands, something would really crack here. The diaper bag is one hundred times heavier than the purple bag. It is the weight, itself, of a child.

"I'll see you in an hour," Marc says, jogging down the steps.

Inside the museum, our second of the day, I ask Berry, "What do you want to see?" She's so much bigger than last time I saw her, but still so small. It's hard to believe that this person, not even as tall as my hip, with wispy hair and baby-round cheeks, is the antagonist in Val's stories. But then she says, "Dinosaurs," scowling at me, eyes narrowed and eyebrows raised, like she can't believe I had the audacity to ask, and honestly, I get it. She's a tough customer.

An unexpected development: the dinosaur halls are temporarily closed for a private event, a fact that the museum is loath to advertise. Val steps aside as her kid flattens herself on the floor, pounding her fists and shrieking. I look around, desperate for some sort of diversion. I start to crouch to floor level, but Val shakes her head. "Just let it run its course," she says. "There's nothing we could possibly do to change this." The security guard looks like he begs to differ, but I choose to believe Val. We stand and watch Berry like we are passengers in an elevator, helplessly tracking the numbers as they light up. Five, four, three, two, one. Berry stands. "Let's go the planetarium," Val says and off we go.

"Do you think she's going to file a police report?" Val asks as we pass through a dim hall, flanked by the taxidermized animals of North America. Berry is focused on a small bag of fruit snacks, not even bothering to look up at the bear, the bobcat, or the moose.

"Berry?" I joke. "She might have a minute ago, but I think she's moved on."

"No, not Berry," she says, nudging me with her shoulder.

"She's already forgotten all about it," I say. "Guaranteed. You snatching her weird empty purse was the least interesting part of her day."

"You're probably right," she says. She swallows hard and I realize my mistake.

Later that week, I'll call Val and claim to have seen an interview with the Movie Star on a late-night show. Which one?

Who knows—all those guys look the same to me, I'll claim, and she'll agree. They do, they all look the same. I wish I could find a clip online, I'll tell her, but I can't. But I wish I could because, guess what—she told the whole story. "That girl had some nerve!" she said. Really? Val will ask. Really, I'll say. I'll be able to picture it, down to the Movie Star's perfect black dress. It will be like it actually happened.

At the planetarium, finally, we discover that there are buttons. It's unclear what they do, exactly, but no matter. Berry stands in front of one and presses it again and again, overcome with delight.

"She's so hopeful," I say.

"You've had a long day," Val says. "You don't have to stay for this."

Do I leave? Of course not. After a while, I start to see it Berry's way. If she pushes that button enough, eventually something might happen.

PARCHED
Taline, 2012

WE WENT TO A DESERT TOWN LAST SUMMER. Stepping out
of the car, I felt underwater—breathless and panicked. I hadn't
known a place could be so hot. In the air-conditioned car, I'd
thought the terrain beautiful, all the hills and red earth, the lacy
shrubs and lazy circles of birds overhead. But I couldn't follow
Mitchell as he strode up the street toward what could only be
described, with its front porch and swinging doors, as a saloon.
I stumbled to the nearest large rock and sat. Next to me, covered by chain link, was a hole in the ground: a mine shaft. The
stone was there to mark it so no one fell. A small sign indicated
that when the mercury market crashed, the cinnabar mine and
adjacent town were abandoned. The town had the saloon, a few
dozen residents, and the workers' derelict quarters; it was a ghost
town, a real-life ghost town. The air had gone wavy with the
heat. Mitchell's outline quivered as he receded—spectral, too.

"Did you ever make it into the saloon?" Louise asks.

"Beer never tasted so good," I tell her. "I remember a high
school teacher explaining to us what the id is by saying it's the

part of you that would do anything for a drink when you're thirsty."

"Didn't you tell me that 'thirsty' is what the kids say now?" Louise says. "The new word for when you're feeling . . ." She raises her eyebrows.

"I guess it's the same thing," I say. "At least it was for Mitchell, right? He was thirsty and he did anything."

I'm on Louise's sofa. It's narrow, mid-century, and dusty rose—stylish but not my first choice for a place to crash. Where else was I supposed to go on a moment's notice, though? Val was upset when I told her I was in a cab on my way here; she thought I should have called her first. But Mitchell is her husband's friend—he introduced us. Not that this is his fault, but why put anyone in that position. I rest my head on a lovely, scratchy throw pillow.

"You can stay as long as you need," Louise says.

I feel the tears mounting, mourning in this moment not for Mitchell but for our apartment. We'd gone domestic in record time, moving in together after only two months. It made terrific financial sense, so no one questioned the decision. Not that they necessarily would have anyway; I think we seemed happy to everyone, not just to ourselves. Our place was sunny and romantic; it had a bay window and a small, light-filled second bedroom. The kitchen was well stocked with everything from vegetables to cocktail mixers. Our books mingled on the shelves.

"I can't believe I'm a couch friend now," I say. "The kind of person that you have to say is 'staying on your couch.' Nothing original about all this." I gesture to my face, which I haven't seen in a while but know all the same is covered in a mess of mascara smears and busted capillaries. And I've been in a constant state of queasiness, puking more than once since it all fell apart—so dramatic, yet so boring.

"No, you're not alone," Louise says, taking a lock of my hair and twisting it between her fingers. "But each heartbreak is singular."

I sit up, looking around for a tissue to blow my nose. "What I couldn't figure out," I say, "is why anyone still lived there. In the ghost town, I mean. Where did they buy their groceries?"

*

At the museum, I gather a group of assistant principals around an artwork by Felix Gonzalez-Torres. I've made the educators happy by providing them with folding stools, by acknowledging that, this being the end of the school year, they must be tired. I am alarmed, in fact, by how happy this makes them: "Thank you, thank you so much," they say, settling onto their stools.

The installation consists of a string of light bulbs hung from the ceiling, pooling in a tangle on a platform near the floor. The light bulbs are the kind we all grew up with—not Edison bulbs, not compact fluorescents—and the wires are white, twinned and entwined. One bulb, six from the top, is dark. The educators look to me to tell them about the work, but instead I set a timer and ask them to sit with it, silently, for three minutes. They squirm for the first minute, but their bodies still by the third. When the alarm trills, they look stunned, their faces bathed in light.

Because they are shy when asked to share their thoughts, I

start with a poll. Who thinks the artwork starts from the top? Half of them raise their hands, and then everyone begins to talk at once. The ones who thought of it as starting from the bottom never would have considered this point as contentious. A member of the first group, an older man with gray hair and an endearingly disheveled appearance, says, "Gravity, right? It comes down from the ceiling."

A woman in a sweater set says, "But it's about heaven. The light is taking us up to the sky."

I sit back, letting them debate until someone finally mentions the darkened bulb. "It's not supposed to be like that," one of them says.

"Of course it is," says another. "This is the most famous museum in the world—they don't have mistakes here." Everyone looks to me again.

"Intentional or not," I say, "what if we came back in a month and more bulbs were out?"

"That's what they do," says the disheveled AP. "Light bulbs die." Everyone gasps.

I share with them some facts about the artist and ask them if or how knowing that he made this work during a time when so many members of his intersecting communities—artists, gay men, people of color—were dying of AIDS, his partner included, and that he himself succumbed to complications soon after making this untitled piece changes their impressions of it. They begin to pull together their thoughts. When someone says, "It's a love story," no one disagrees.

Since they are educators and this is a professional development session, I get meta. "What did I do there?" I ask. No one seems to have an answer. "What I was doing felt sort of beside the point, right?"

I don't mean that I didn't do anything, I tell them. What I mean is that I orchestrated a conversation from which I could be absent. What I mean is that, while I am happy to share with them what I know, my thoughts and opinions don't have more value than theirs. It takes courage to step back and relinquish control of the conversation, but we can learn to trust the art and each other. I mean the lesson to be: Listen. Provide space. Believe in your students and their ability to be profound. But they wipe their eyes and look at me like they've been tricked.

*

Mitchell is in Louise's galley kitchen when I get back that evening. She fusses with the hem of her sweater, and I mouth, semi-joking, "Traitor." Val would have punched him in the face, not let him into her apartment. Louise retreats to her bedroom, although she leaves the door ajar. In her defense, Mitchell claims that he convinced her I knew he was coming. I lean on the marble counter, arms crossed; he stands against the fridge, a hanging basket of bananas and onions skimming his shoulder. A bit of onionskin drifts onto his pink button-down shirt. I grab it, crinkling it between my fingers. I think of another Felix Gonzalez-Torres piece: Hundreds of shiny wrapped hard candies the exact weight of his partner, Ross, piled in the corner of a gallery. Visitors select and eat the candies, the pile dwindling, wasting away, and eventually disappearing. Years after both of their deaths, the artwork is remade again and again, all over the world. That's love. The onionskin disintegrates between my fingers. What is this?

But assistant principals be damned, I practice what I preach. I look Mitchell in his big brown eyes and wait.

"If anything," he says, "I should be the one to move out."

I chew on my lip, cross and uncross my arms. He's right, but I never want to go to that apartment again.

"I mean, I don't think either of us should move. Like I said, it was stupid and I'm so sorry." He must have practiced his speech. "But, I mean, we've been together over two years. We made it through, you know. It was hard, but we did it. What about, you know, starting a family?"

I turn to look over my shoulder at the cracked bedroom door, making sure Louise is getting this. Her mouth is agape. He's referring to a miscarriage—or not quite referring to it, since he can't even say what he's talking about—that I don't think we did make it through. As far as I know, he wasn't cheating on me before it happened. It was early, and I felt like I took it well given how much I wanted that pregnancy. He seemed okay, too, or so I thought. That we had been cleared by the doctor to start trying again, well, I'm not mean enough to say it, not even to him, but I can only be thankful it hasn't worked.

"Are you not talking to me?" he asks. "Isn't that sort of childish?"

Louise's knives are lined up next to me, neat in their wooden block. I wouldn't want to go that route, though. I open the drawer closest to me, looking for one of those metal skewers like my mom uses to grill kabobs. I don't know why Louise would have one, grill-less as she is, but that's the tool that would do it: I could slip it into his ear and scramble—unscramble?—his brain. Didn't he used to be a reasonable person, a man who loved me? In the absence of a skewer, I pluck the closest thing she seems to have, one of those little corncob holders itself shaped like a cob of corn. I turn it over in my hand.

"You want to know who it is, right?" he says. His eyes are watery. Could he have lost weight in the space of three days? He looks skinnier. That there are so many contenders in my mind makes it somehow less essential that I have the real information. That I think it could have been any one of a number of women says more than enough.

Later, Louise asks, "Did he say 'is'?"

*

Louise is going to a gala for work and brings me along. Because, as I stormed out of my apartment, I didn't think to pack anything gala-ready, I am wearing an old bridesmaid dress of hers. She kept insisting that her regular dresses would fit me, but no, I knew I needed to find that one from the summer she had a sprained ankle and gained a little weight in the absence of her usual stringent workout routine. The result is that she looks chic and put-together in a tight, mid-calf black number and I'm oddly Grecian, in yellow chiffon. My mother always claimed our heritage precluded us from wearing yellow, that it would make our skin look too green, but Louise works wonders with her makeup kit.

We wander through the cocktail hour in a former bank, ogling Corinthian columns and accepting champagne refills. My stomach is acting up, churning more with each drink, but

I keep taking them. Louise is a different person in this context, as the room starts to fill with her fashion colleagues. I watch her toss off air-kiss after air-kiss, name-drop after name-drop, do a thing with her phone where she shoots her contact information through space into someone else's, a trick I didn't know possible. Even her posture is different as she balances in her heels. She calls her career in hipster hosiery "fashion adjacent," but it looks to me like she fits in here.

Across the room, I think I see Carl Lucas, a photographer who was on a panel at the museum last year. I nudge Louise and she confirms, although she calls him a fashion photographer. I picture his work, sort of voyeuristic street photography; he catches people in moments of tension, anxiety, or awkwardness. In my favorite image, a mother and teenage daughter lean toward each other—they look alike, the rounded shape of their noses, the angle of their brows, the way they hold their arms slightly back as they yell—furious and full of spite, but the photograph also has a tenderness to it. I can't believe an artist like him has a day job, but on the other hand—it's New York—of course I can.

I follow Louise around, wondering if I should go to talk to Carl, engaging in an internal debate until it is time to sit down at our table for dinner.

The first speech is self-congratulatory and dull; I am not sure who or what is being fêted, if we are raising money tonight or merely celebrating. My fish is mealy and bland, terrible enough that I wonder if the caterers just assumed, with this crowd, no one would be eating anyway.

I slip out, tottering in Louise's too-high, half-size-too-small heels, to find the ladies' room. It is down a set of slippery marble stairs; I grip the railing to keep from hobbling myself. Carl Lucas is at the bottom, watching the show.

"One cocktail too many?" he asks.

I shake my head. "Bad in heels."

He steps aside so I can pass, but I touch his elbow.

"Wait," I say. "I know your work. I really like it." I explain about the panel and that one photograph I think of often. He leans back against the wall and looks me up and down. It seems like he's deciding if he wants to talk based more on aesthetics than on what I said. Honestly, that doesn't surprise me. At the museum, I can stand for hours in the Minimalist galleries surrounded by the work of notorious misogynists and misanthropes—murderers, even—enraptured by the way the goddamn beautiful art makes me reconsider sculpture's relationship to the floor. Mitchell never got why I liked that stuff, which is funny because it turns out he's just like them, without the brilliance and bluster. Actually, he's not like them—he's simply a jerk, too. Carl adjusts his orange plastic-framed glasses, then pulls a flask from the inside pocket of his jacket, swigs, and offers it to me.

"There are free drinks here, you know," I say.

"But not, like, right here," he says.

I can't tell if we're flirting, or if he hates me, or if I likely hate him. Should I lean closer? Should we make out? Should he say, You wanna get out of here?

As he swills from his flask, I notice he is older than I thought he was, maybe fifty or so. There are streaks of gray running through his pushed-back chin-length hair. The impressive camera hanging around his neck rests on the slightest paunch. "You been up on the catwalk here?" he asks.

"First time gala-goer," I say. "I don't walk a lot of catwalks."

"Want to use the bathroom first?" he asks, which I think is strange until I realize that is what I was coming down here to do.

"It was just an excuse to get out of there," I say, nodding my head back toward the party. He places his hand on my hip and guides me to another, narrower set of stairs just past the restroom doors. I resist the urge to shrug him off because it does help me to keep steady. I'm still too wobbly, though. I have to pause and remove my shoes. The marble is cool on my cramped feet. He smirks. I say, "Dude, you're here in jeans and a leather jacket."

We make our way up what feels like a hundred flights of stairs, like we are mounting some mythical castle tower. When we finally emerge, it is onto a narrow walkway rimming the room where the party is being held. The track lights are just below us, as are the pulls for the red velvet curtains. *This* is the kind of catwalk he meant. From up here, the tables and the chairs fanned out around them look like sunflowers, and the disorder of plates and silverware and glasses upon glasses of wine like sequins sparkling. There's a wrought iron railing holding us back from quite a fall. The colors below swirl as the shapes distend and retract.

"Are you afraid of heights?" Carl asks, leaning over the railing to snap pictures.

If he'd asked me while we were still in the basement, I would have said no, but I have to catch my breath before answering. I rub my arms. "I think a little," I say. It's that desert town feeling.

"Sit," he says. "Ground yourself." I gather my sunny chiffon skirt and slide down the wall, sitting cross-legged on the catwalk.

"Better?" he asks.

I close my eyes, breathing as best I can. When my heart quiets, I open my eyes again, licking my lips to unstick them from my teeth so I can answer him. He isn't waiting for my answer, though; he is taking pictures. I feel a little better. I keep most of my body pressed to the wall but crane my neck forward, and, working backward from the podium where the speeches are still happening, pinpoint where Louise is sitting. I can tell it's her from the tense, birdlike way she holds her shoulders, but I can't see much else from so high. "I see my friend," I say.

"Point her out," Carl says, stepping back toward me, and I do. He trains his camera on her, performs some adjustments, *clicks, clicks, clicks*, looks at his screen, and does it again.

He crouches, his knees straining against the tight fabric of his jeans. "Look," he says. He shows me the image on the screen. I see Louise with remarkable clarity. In her elegant black dress, she is perched at the edge of her chair, looking toward the bathroom stairs, her napkin twisted in her two hands. Everyone else seated at her table is nebulous, blurry to her sharp focus, their edges permeable, laughing at whoever is at the podium. Louise looks apart, separate from the crowd. He's isolated her, but also identified her; she looks raw, herself. It is a photograph to make a hundred assistant principals cry.

"How did you do that?" I ask.

"Art is hard to talk about," he says.

"It's easy to talk about," I counter, shaking my head. "Easy to set on fire."

He looks at me for a long moment, as if he's trying to parse the metaphor. But there's no metaphor. When I lit that match and held it to my painting, I really did want to see what would happen. Would the canvas burn evenly, or would the flames follow the path of the paint? When it was clear that it was just going to burn, to be reduced to ash, I'd been disappointed. I'd thought, Another failed experiment. What I hadn't counted on were the sprinklers going off. I don't tell people that that's what actually destroyed my work and got me evicted. It was water, not fire. I wonder if Carl will take my picture, but he doesn't.

"I need to go," I say. He holds my hand, helping me inch my way back to the stairs. Before I descend, I say, "If I give you my email, will you send me that photo of her?"

"Doesn't work like that," he says.

*

Safe and steady at ground level, I slip my feet back into Louise's shoes and give her a little wave as I return to my seat. Her relief takes the shape of a full body sigh. "Where, what, why?" she whispers.

"Carl Lucas," I say.

Her eyes widen. "Thirsty?" she asks. She reaches her clammy hand out to squeeze mine. "I told you the yellow dress would be okay."

As impossible as it seems, the speeches are still ongoing when dessert is served. I spoon vanilla panna cotta, my gaze drifting skyward, toward the catwalk. The lights lining it are so bright I can barely look. But I do. I close my eyes, watching the blue-purple afterimage dance behind my eyelids. When I open them, one of the bulbs is out. I can't remember—was it always like that? I shift my focus: the rest of the bulbs are still burning strong.

JESUS LOUISE
Louise, 2013

THE GOAT NECK ARRIVES AT THE TABLE LOOKING more like itself than Louise expected. The tacos are DIY, it turns out, so rather than a tangle of shredded meat that could quickly be wrapped in its warm, round delivery device and dispatched into her mouth, the protein is still intact, cylindrical and headless, balanced on a wooden plank beside a stack of steaming tortillas and five little dishes of assorted salsas and crunchy elements.

Clive needles the point of his knife into the meat, wriggling it until a chunk comes loose. Is it the spine that is now exposed? "I sort of want the restaurant to do the cooking for me at this price, you know?" he says. "This is a lot of work."

Louise watches as he assembles what looks like a fantastic taco, the meat crowned with red and green sauces and a sprinkle of pickled radish. She extends her hand.

He eyes her palm, the taco, her. "Because this is a first date, Louise," he says, passing it to her. "And only because."

She polishes it off in a few bites. "My compliments to the chef," she says, wiping the grease from her fingers.

"At least you give credit where credit is due." He pops his own taco in his mouth, finally. He closes his eyes as he chews. "Oh yeah," he says.

They trade first date stories, surely a faux pas, but better than running out of things to say. She tells him about a guy from last week who, when faced with a pool of sediment at the bottom of his wine glass, cried actual tears. "'I'm so sick of getting the dregs,' he said. And I was like, 'Well, excuse me.'"

"I went out with this girl who seemed a little glassy-eyed," Clive says. "Turns out she had norovirus. I was on the toilet for like three days after that date."

Louise separates a juicy chunk of goat flesh from its bone, squeamishness gone. "I have to ask, did you make out with the norovirus girl? To have gotten so sick?"

"I don't kiss and tell," he says, then cocks his head, mischievous. "But, I do fuck on the first date."

Louise nods over his shoulder toward the restaurant bathroom. "Should we, then?"

He hesitates, licking a drop of tomatillo off his thumb. She smiles—closed-mouthed in case there's anything in her teeth—watching him struggle to decide if she's joking. Honestly, if she could get her hands on a toothbrush first, she would do it. Clive has that most reviled of hairstyles, his long, dark locks gathered into a knot on top of his head, but his jeans and denim button-down fit him so well he must get his clothes tailored, and, unless he is some sort of internet imposter, he seems to be the documentarian behind a film that inspired her to donate real money to a cause after seeing it last year.

They eat the spicy chocolates that come with the bill, and he pays. This is something she allows when the income imbalance is clear—a banker, doctor, or lawyer will always pay. A teacher? She offers to pick it up, and usually they split. She doesn't know with a semi-successful filmmaker, so she assumes the best of his wallet.

Outside on the sidewalk, the night is balmy, and Clive invites her to hear his friend Frogger's jazz band perform, a thing it seems they are doing a few blocks away. She pulls her hand through her hair. A goat neck she can abide, but not jazz, not a friend with a hilarious name. They make out on the street corner for a few minutes, until the angle gets too tough—he is tall enough that she really has to crane to get to his mouth—and then they say their good nights. "I'll text you," he says.

*

The next morning, Louise walks to her brother and sister-in-law's apartment. Céleste buzzes her up; she wants to hear about the date. "My stories are all the same," Louise says. "Don't you get sick of them?"

"Sick*er*?" she asks, raising the ridge where her eyebrows used to be.

Louise swats her arm, a thing she wouldn't have done a few months ago, but Céleste responded well to treatment and is getting better now—she thinks. Céleste makes the occasional dry cancer joke, but actual information is hard to come by from either her or Louise's brother. Louise can never tell if Eddie's protecting Céleste's privacy or if he really doesn't know what the hell is going on either. Because Louise can't help but picture him as his fourteen-year-old self still, she feels like it's the latter, but because he is actually thirty-four at this point, and a man who loves his wife, it is probably the former. Poor Eddie—he's a true high-powered account executive at the kind of advertising firm people work their whole lives to join, and Louise still laughs when she sees him in his three-thousand-dollar suits.

"I think I like him," Louise says. "It's hard to tell after one date, but the banter was good."

"You've heard from him since?" Céleste asks.

Louise tells her no, although she has, a 4 a.m. *u up?* text, which obviously she should hold against him, but what the hell. If she had been up, she would have told him to come over.

They are sitting in Céleste and Eddie's perfect kitchen, on these little red chairs that contrast brightly with the black-and-white tiled floor. Sunlight filters in past the leafy plants hanging in the window. Céleste pours coffee from her antiquated yet charming stovetop system. By chance, they live a few blocks from each other in the East Village; Louise started stopping by mornings after her brother left for work and before she had to, when Céleste was alone, weak and miserable. Now that she's getting stronger, Louise has kept it up, maybe more for herself than her sister-in-law. Describing these mornings once to Valerie, Louise explained, "Céleste grinds the coffee beans herself, every time. It's because she's French, and because she is better than me." The coffee is smooth yet strong. Sometimes Louise still can't believe Céleste is with her brother.

"Do you have to work today?" Céleste asks.

Louise does, of course she does, but if she wanted to take a half day off, she is the person who approves the request. If someone wanted to complain about her coming in late, she is the person they would complain to. "*Comme ci, comme ça,*" she answers.

"That's not how you use that phrase," Céleste says. "But if you're not doing anything else, would you come to the doctor with me? Just for a conversation, nothing graphic."

She pronounces it graph*ique*.

"Sure," Louise says. The first few times they met, Louise wasn't convinced that Céleste even remembered her name, so she can't help but thrill at Céleste's every gesture toward her. At this point, a few years in, she does think Céleste enjoys her company, but she's still waiting to be taken into her confidence, to be made her *friend*.

Céleste slips her feet into black flats, ties her voluminous taupe sweater around her slight middle, and adjusts the rose-and-tan scarf she has turbaned around her head. Louise had thought she was just coming over for a coffee fix before running home to shower and get dressed for real. She follows her sister-in-law out the door in the white T-shirt she slept in, day-three hair. She isn't like this. She's usually clean and intentional, but that all falls apart when she's around Céleste.

On the subway, Louise is too distracted by the fact that no one on the packed train offers Céleste a seat to pay much attention to where they're going. "None of these jerks think you might be feeling a little tired?"

Céleste rolls her eyes, which are a shade of brown so cool they're almost gray, and strange without their lashes. "*I* gave my seat to a woman carrying a sleeping toddler the other day," she says. "She didn't want to take it, but she needed it more than I did."

Louise wants to say aloud, loud enough that they hear, that she hopes all these people get cancer, but she doesn't know if Céleste would appreciate that. She follows her out of the station and across the street into a building that seems to be filled with high-end beauty salons, spas, and appointment-only boutiques.

They exit the elevator and head down a long well-lit hall-way, then veer right when most everyone else veers left, to pass through the frosted-glass door of an OB-GYN office. Louise assumed they were going to Céleste's oncologist, but if she had stopped to think about it, she would have realized that they are nowhere near the hospital and adjacent offices where Cé-leste and Eddie have spent so much time this past year. Louise twists the hem of her shirt, lingering near the doorway, not sure what she's doing here. She sinks into a plush leather couch— this is clearly a fancy office—while Céleste checks in with the receptionist. There is a young woman across from her leafing through an old *US Weekly*, and a couple, probably in their early forties, off in the corner. The woman is hugely pregnant and sipping from a cup of tea.

Céleste finishes at the counter and comes to sit next to Louise, but not quite as close as would be normal. She looks down, twisting her wedding ring around and around.

"You didn't want to bring Eddie?" Louise asks.

"They told me to bring someone," she says. "Who, they didn't specify." Her sentences have so many z's in them, some-times she sounds like a cartoon of a French person. A nurse peeks out from behind a wall and calls in the couple. The man helps the woman to her feet. They both have light hair with some gray mixed in. They are all smiles. Céleste peers at them, then back down at her lap. When the nurse comes to call her name, Louise stands up, too. Then Céleste finally looks right at her. "Will you wait here instead?" she asks.

Louise is even less sure now what she's doing here but slides back onto the couch as Céleste disappears down the hall. She clicks around on her phone, scrolling through her calendar wondering when the last time she went to the gyno was and if she's due for an appointment. Since Val got an IUD after giving birth and convinced her to get one, too, she doesn't have pills to re-up, so it is easier to lose track. That's about the only downside, though—she should have gotten an IUD years ago. All of the birth control, none of the hassle? She doesn't know why it wasn't fashionable when she was twenty-two, or twelve for that matter.

A family enters the waiting room, a mother and two little girls, maybe four and eight. For a moment Louise wonders why they're not in school but then sees the mom has a whole box of tissues poking out of her purse and the skin under the kids' noses is a bright, raw red. Appointments at this office must be hard to come by for her not to have canceled rather than tow two sick kids along with her. Louise makes a note to whisk Céleste quickly past them when she comes out. Germs are the last thing she needs. The nurse is kind enough to beckon the mother right into the back. The receptionist says she'll keep an eye on the kids; their mother issues a string of stern admonishments and behavior instructions. The little girls are wearing the same black-and-white-striped tights, but the younger one is wearing a pink tutu-like tunic over them, while the older one is in a more subdued long lavender sweater. They have blunt, unevenly cut black bangs and smooth, dreamy skin. The older one sees Louise looking at them, then slaps her sister's knees together, pulling her tunic down to cover her crotch. Louise hadn't realized it had been exposed.

She keeps her eyes trained on her phone but can't help listening to the girls in conversation. "Yellow and blue," the big one says. "You mix them together and you get green."

"Purple," the little one says.

"For purple, you mix blue and red," her sister tells her.

"Purple and purple, you make purple," the little one says. She hears the big one sigh, as if she wants to help her understand, but she's just not up to the task. She raps her sister on the knee again, reminding her to keep her legs together.

After a short while, Céleste is back. She taps Louise on the shoulder when Louise doesn't notice her standing there. She is paler than when she went in, with redder eyes. She looks like a person to whom something has happened.

"Shit," Louise says. The little girls giggle.

Céleste glances at them, nods. "Shit," she says.

*

Outside, even now, Céleste takes the lead. They wind up in a bookstore café. It seems like it would be the quietest kind of café, but instead, it is buzzing—people meeting over laptops, waving paperbacks at each other, sucking tall drinks through straws. It is cozy, with dark wood walls and the musty smell of old paper. Louise takes Céleste's order and buys them both espressos. While they're being brewed, she sees Céleste look at her phone, put it facedown on the wobbly table in front of her, pick it up again, put it back down. Louise adds a drop of milk to each of their drinks, christening them what Céleste calls *noisettes.*

"*Parfait,*" Céleste says. She accepts hers and takes a sip. "So, you've guessed what the doctor told me?"

The smell of the coffee makes Louise's heart rush; she's already had too much. Her own middle aches, vicariously, for Céleste's annexed body parts.

Louise shakes her head. It seems better not to guess.

"When I went the first time, I barely knew where I was. There have been so many appointments. It wasn't until they called me to come in to speak about the results that I really thought about it. What it meant to go to a fertility special- ist." She pushes back the cuticle on her thumb. "Eddie doesn't know that I went," she continues, "let alone what they said. I don't think I can tell him. He's going to be so upset."

Louise waits for her to say more. When she doesn't, Louise bites her lip. "Are you asking me to tell him? Is that why you wanted me to come? What . . . what did they say?" Eddie is her *brother,* for goodness' sake. Knowing something serious that he doesn't is not the kind of confidence she'd wished for.

"*Jésus,* Louise," Céleste says, without a breath of *Jeez Louise* about it. In French, the rhyme doesn't play out. "No. I only wanted you to come because I didn't know how I'd react. If I'd need help getting home. I had a feeling what they would say." She takes Louise's coffee from her and finishes it, like she's throwing back tequila shots.

"And?" she presses when Céleste doesn't continue.

"She wanted to tell me about all the other ways to make a family." Céleste flutters her lashless eyes. "Don't say anything."

Louise nods. A funny thing is how, after Céleste got sick, Eddie and Louise's parents got back together. They'd been living apart for a few years, their dad in a condo across town. Their mother told her that, seeing Eddie in pain, they knew no one would understand how they felt besides the other. "Except me," Louise had said, but her mother shook her head.

"No, I don't mean now. I mean to Eddie," Céleste says. "Don't tell him."

Louise agrees. Of course she does.

*

At work, she tries to catch up on the morning emails she missed, but she's distracted by everything—the internet, the streaks she never noticed on the office windows, the tapping of other people's fingers on their keyboards. She has this one sliver of a first memory: wiping drool from the soft, glistening folds of Eddie's double chin with a cotton cloth, their mother telling her what a gentle big sister she was, encouraging her into that tenderness.

Because she has to tell someone about Céleste and Eddie, about Céleste not telling Eddie, Louise calls Valerie. "Don't see him alone," she offers as advice. "Don't see either of them for a while if you can help it. And maybe when things calm down, you should tell her that it was inappropriate to ask you to keep a secret like this." Valerie, like so many good friends, gives advice she herself probably would not follow.

*

All afternoon and evening, Louise picks up the phone and puts it down. She almost does it at ten o'clock. She almost does it at eleven. Finally, she gives in just before midnight. She sends the text.

The response, though not immediate, comes within ten minutes: *I am.*

Before she gets in the cab, she stops at the taco truck that parks a few blocks away. She decides on four tacos: two carnitas, two barbacoa. They are warm in her lap and smell savory with a little sharpness from the lime.

The way she expects it to go, Clive will toss the bag of food aside as he throws her down on his bed. Maybe they will tear—famished—at the tacos after, or maybe they'll just be something to laugh over, maybe he'll find them in the morning and wonder if they're still okay to eat. But when he opens the door, clad in low-slung lavender yoga pants and a black sleeveless T-shirt, he is definitely interested in taking the tacos before taking Louise.

When, mouth full, he finally offers her one, she demurs, saying she already had dinner, though actually she hasn't. She just thinks she'll be better at this whole thing on an empty stomach. If this whole thing happens, in the end. Although why would she be here otherwise? They've already joked about fucking on the first date; she's already received a middle-of-the-night proposition. They're dealing in inevitabilities, in biding time until she doesn't have to think about anything.

They're on his couch, which is a soft, warm leather, probably expensive enough to rival the one at the doctor's office today. If appearances can be believed, before she arrived he was curled up on it under a blanket, reading a novel. On the wall behind them, framed amid the design posters, is an award from a documentary festival in Montreal for the movie it seems he really did make.

After he finishes his two tacos, all the while amiable and chatting as if they're old buddies, telling her about Frogger's jazz performance last night, how she should have come, Clive wipes his face on a small paper napkin and says, "I'm surprised you texted. I wouldn't have guessed you would, you know, follow up."

"If I had been up when you texted me last night, I would have answered then. So really you were the one to follow up."

He reaches to adjust his hair. It is very dark and shiny—a lot like Céleste's hair used to be. Louise wonders if Céleste's will grow in like that again or if it will be different, curlier or straighter. Clive's large, silt-colored eyes, too, are like hers in a way. Louise asks him, "Are you French?" at the same time as he says, "What text?"

She entreats him to look at his phone and he reddens when he does. "Frogger and I went shot for shot," he says.

"I don't know if a less sexy sentence has ever been spoken," Louise says, and he leans in to kiss her. It's easier than last night since they're both sitting. Her neck doesn't hurt.

In his bedroom—hardwood floors and clean cotton sheets on his crisp, tucked-in queen bed—she raises her arms over her head so he can pull off her sweater. She is not sorry to see his purple stretchy pants disappear into the corner.

His hands glance over her and come to rest on her hips. It's working—she's distracted, she's in the moment, she's marveling at the softness, the strangeness, of the human earlobe. She doesn't have to ask after a condom—he plucks one from a cut-glass box on his side table.

But then she thinks: What use are these hips to me? What if I could turn this fleeting encounter into what Céleste and Eddie can't have, what Eddie doesn't know he can't have? The baby would have Eddie's dimpled limbs and round cheeks, Céleste's lustrous hair and her dark eyes. Céleste is my sister now. She is saying *purple and purple makes purple*, and it's what I have to do: sigh, take care of her, and wait for her to understand that no, it is red and blue.

Louise sighs. If she could, she would have the baby, she would hand her over.

Clive tilts her head up, his index finger under her chin. "Are you okay?" he asks.

"Me?" she says. "I'm fine." She closes her eyes; she arches her back. She stays the night.

SEAS BETWEEN US
Taline, 2012

It is New Year's Eve and I'm in the backseat of an SUV, wearing an ill-fitting sequin shell pilfered from my mother's closet, watching the familiar sights of my hometown fly by out the window. We haven't started partying yet—if that is what we'll be doing tonight—but Zoe's husband, Brian, is already taking curves fast enough to send the case of champagne on the floor next to me careening into my legs.

"Whose house are we going to again?" I ask, rubbing my calf.

"Dean Holt's," Brian says, as if that means anything to me. "I work with him."

I don't remember where Brian works. He used to do something with sports, baseball, I think, but after Zoe put up a fuss about his hours, he changed careers. When I'm in Jersey to catch up with Zoe, the few times a year we still manage to make a plan—usually the diner and disco fries—we talk about their two kids, or the latest season of whatever silly reality show we both watch, or the dumb things we did in high school; Brian's job must be dull enough that it doesn't warrant much mention. Still, it's been years now; I can't exactly ask what he does.

He continues, "Did Zoe tell you about the party?"

"Of course," I say. "How would I have known about it otherwise?"

"Not that there is a party," Brian says. "But, like, what kind of party it is."

"I just wanted her to stay up past midnight!" Zoe says, laughing. It's true; I'm visiting my mother for the holidays, but she's at a party, too. I declined her invite, planning to call it a night at 10 p.m. That sounded fine to me.

It is dark here in the suburbs, without much even in the way of lamps to illuminate the street. Sitting in the backseat, all I can see of my friend and her husband are their silhouetted heads and pleasant profiles when they turn slightly to address me.

"Where's Mitch tonight?" Brian asks, raising his eyebrows at me in the rearview.

I make eye contact with my own reflection in the window, searching my memory for what I told Zoe. I won't be able to keep it up much longer, this ruse that we're still together. It just felt good to me, somehow, having this one place—between me and Zoe—where that life I thought I'd had was still intact. It's not the first time I've lied to her about a relationship ending, but I guess I haven't learned any lessons. "The last person you want around on New Year's Eve is Mitchell," I say. "He'd start talking about how time is a construct or something." Brian and Zoe exchange a look, but neither of them presses me for more.

Although we don't drive for long, we enter and exit at least two highways, so when we pull up in front of an overgrown mansion, a monstrosity of new construction, I have no idea what town we're in. There's a circular driveway that is, despite the size of the house, totally unnecessary in its grandeur, and a dry marble fountain in the middle of it. "I know," Zoe says when we step out of the car and she sees my face. "These are not exactly your people."

"But he's *good* people," Brian says. He lifts his chin toward the front door as he hoists the case of champagne out of the backseat. "I've known this kid a long time."

I don't know what it is that makes grown men here insist on calling each other "kid."

Zoe wiggles out of her winter coat, revealing a tiny red dress. When we were younger, we would joke that she was so flat she couldn't look trashy no matter what she wore, whereas I, with my F cups, could make a cardigan suggestive. This dress she's got on almost disproves our theory, though. She's not wearing a bra under it—how could she, with straps that thin and a V-neck that low—and in the cold, her nipples are borderline obscene. Also, after the kids, her breasts are not as small as they used to be. It's nice to see her feeling so confident, but it's confusing. Destabilizing. I'm used to seeing her in capri pants and tees. "Leave your coat in the car," she says. "Believe me, you don't want it piled on the bed in there."

"They could have a coatroom with a house this size, no?" I ask, but I do as I'm told. "Am I going to know anyone here? I'd rather not ring in the New Year with anyone else from high school." I'll never understand how it is that Zoe purports to feel the very same way I do about all the terrible girls we went to school with, yet still chooses to live among them.

"I can't promise that," she says.

"Give her the thing," Brian says. They exchange a look, eyes mischievous and bright, and even on their wedding day, I don't think I've seen them seem more in love. I breathe through a pang of jealousy. From her incongruous floral quilted shoulder bag, Zoe extracts a handful of fur and ribbed knits. A sweater, thank goodness.

"I was going to say," I start, "that dress could use a little—" But then she untangles the mass and hands a mask to Brian. Then one to me. Then she puts hers on.

These aren't sexy masquerade masks; those I could handle. Over her head, Zoe unfurls what I think at first is a white balaclava. It is fuzzy and completely obscures her face, her hair, and even her neck. When she straightens it out, it comes into focus: a polar bear. It is part of a costume: from the neck down, she is a human woman, but from the neck up, she's like a strange ursine bank robber. The mask has holes for her eyes and mouth but is plush, with ears and a snout. Brian's mask is just as startling: he is a panther, maybe, black and feline, more menacing than a cat. And mine—how ridiculous—it is a flamingo: pink, with a black-and-yellow crocheted beak.

"I'll just call a car to take me home," I say, handing her back the mask.

"Good luck with that on New Year's Eve," Zoe says, her voice slightly muffled. "It'll take forever. This isn't the city, you know!"

"I'll call Val, then," I say. Val would drop everything to come save me, even on New Year's Eve. I know she, Marc, and Berry have a tradition now, just the three of them, where they blow noisemakers and watch the countdown at 7 p.m., midnight London time. But Berry is probably in bed now, or almost—Val could leave her with Marc.

But I've left my phone in my coat pocket, which is locked in the car. I tell Zoe I need to get it and she says, "Phones are frowned upon at this party." She grabs my elbow and starts maneuvering me toward the path to the door, which is intricately tiled and lined with twinkling fairy lights.

Brian snatches the flamingo mask from Zoe and, from behind, wraps a thick arm around my shoulders. I'm used to Mitchell's arms, which are barely more substantial than mine. Before I can wrestle out of his grasp, he stretches it over my head.

It's warm, I'll give it that. There are eyeholes so I can see the night unobstructed, but my nose and mouth are covered. The yarn is porous enough, but it's a little itchy, and it's so close, and there's a tightness in my chest. I try to take a deep breath; the December chill seeps further into me. I'm here because it's hard to say no to Zoe, and because I didn't want my mother to think I'm as sad as I am, but in the stale yarn of the mask, I can almost smell the comfort of the sheets on my childhood bed, laundered hundreds of times and waiting for me a few miles away. I say, "Zoe?" but she doesn't answer because Brian is already at the door, holding it open for us to follow him in.

*

The foyer is filled with shiny white marble, overhung by a crystal chandelier the size of a small boat, its lights dimmed. Poinsettias and sprigs of pine line the stairs leading up from both sides of the entryway. Soft jazz, the scratching of forks on plates, and the pop of a bottle come from somewhere just beyond where I can see. The ambience is a far cry from the costume parties Val and I gladly attended in college. It would seem very adult, if not for the presence of the ridiculous masks. I want to text Val; I reach for my phantom phone. Zoe grabs my searching hand and squeezes as she and Brian start toward the arched doorway leading to—what? She lets go and, although I tell myself it is only my cold hand, not my head or my heart that misses Mitchell, my palm does feel it.

We round a corner and there it is: the party. Everyone's face is somehow concealed. It seems clear that this is the point of the masks—not to dress up but to hide who's beneath. Two men hovering by the sink are luchadores from the neck up, expensive suits from the neck down. They sip drinks, metal straws poking through garish mouth holes; one of them draws circles with his finger on the wrist of a woman wearing what looks to be a koala head. Dotted here and there are people in plain black ski masks, even more disturbing than the strangely deflated-looking sloth nuzzling a man dressed as a lizard, or the woman with iridescent fish scales covering her face, scalp, and neck. The fish approaches me as I stand, suddenly alone, not sure where Zoe and Brian have gone. She presses a real crystal glass into my hand, filled to the top with champagne, and I see the flurry of pink feathers around my head reflected a thousand times over in her scales. "How am I supposed to drink this?" I ask. I have to repeat myself twice for her to understand me through the layers and layers of fabric between my mouth and her ear.

She laughs when my question finally gets across, and I can see all the muscles in her face that are involved in the action, the scales lighting them up in a way that is practically cyborgian. She plucks one of the metal straws from a vase on the marble counter.

"Of everything that seems wrong with this picture," I say, drawing my hand across the room, "nothing seems quite as bad as drinking champagne through a straw."

She laughs again. "Is this not the night you had planned?"

New Year's Eve, for the past couple of years, has been me and Mitchell in our apartment, a bottle of something pricey, a pile of meticulously poached shrimp and a bowl of spicy cocktail sauce, a handful of friends crowded around, digging in. "I didn't have a plan," I tell the fish-woman. For a moment, I think that if I'd known in advance that we'd need masks for this, I could have made a great one. I wouldn't have, though—had Zoe told me our plans for this evening, I just would have declined.

"You came with Zoe and Brian tonight, right?" she says.

"How on earth could you tell?" I ask.

"I just could," she says. "Brian has a particular gait. I do occupational therapy, so I notice those things."

"I guess I thought the masks were supposed to make everyone anonymous?" I run my index finger beneath mine, wiping a few beads of sweat from my neck.

"It's more the illusion of anonymity."

I like this fish-woman. She seems like she actually could be "my people." I ask, "Is this your house?"

"I wish," she says. "Isn't it beautiful? Here's Dean." She wraps her arm around the waist of a man who appears with a platter of canapés balanced on his forearm. She apologizes quickly for using his name, but he shrugs it off.

"Everyone knows me," he says. His build, with his great tapering torso and his enormous, furred lion mask, is so on the nose. He hooks his thumb into the waistband of the fish's tight white jeans. I might take a smoked salmon tart from the plate he proffers, but how would I eat it? No one else has removed their mask.

"I hope you're enjoying the spread," Dean says, his voice booming though his lion muzzle. He's practiced at making himself heard.

"You must be a beast in the boardroom," I say to him. I jam the top of my metal straw through the gaps in my knit beak, suck down champagne. I try to see if I can reset my brain. Would it be possible to find this fun? No, my brain screams, absolutely not.

Then Zoe is at my elbow saying, "Oh good, you've met."

I think that we haven't really, but the fact that Dean didn't ask me about myself? I'm okay with that.

"Sorry we lost you," she says as the others disperse. "We had to drop the champagne out back. He serves the good stuff first and then, when that runs dry, brings in ours." She laughs and clinks her glass against mine. "It is good, right? Make sure you try the food, too. To die for."

I take her wrist in my hand. I'd like to look her in the eye, but there's too much fluff to make it work. I ask her, "Why would you bring me here?"

"I thought it would be fun," she says after a pause. "You used to go to costume parties all the time, right? I remember seeing the pictures of you and Valerie all dressed up. I wanted to do that with you, too, you know? I feel like we never hang out anymore."

"Oh," I say. My grip on her wrist softens. It's very like Zoe to twist things around so I go from being annoyed to feeling bad before I even know what happened. "Okay. I hear you. But—this particular party? I mean."

She laughs. Giggles, really. "This party is legendary around here. It sort of gets passed down, you know? I think our parents used to go to one just like it when we were kids! Can you imagine? And it should be *extra* fun for you, because you aren't on the PTA with any of these people."

"But you know I'd never, don't you?" I say. I lean back against a table covered in discarded glasses. It's so heavy it doesn't wobble under my weight. "Under any circumstances, really, but I mean, I'd never cheat on Mitchell."

"I do know that," Zoe says. Her tone shifts after I use the word *cheat* in a way not everyone would notice. She glances around us, taking in the swirl of party guests that ebbs and flows through the foyer, where we've migrated as we talk. She must be checking for Brian, making sure he's out of earshot in case I say anything incriminating. It was only after she'd made a big show of forgiving me for sleeping with Colin that I found out that he did, in fact, try to get with her immediately after I ended things. She really forgave me, I think, because she got to keep the moral high ground from every angle. She continues, "But I also know he's not in Florida with his grandmother, or even if he is . . ."

It's funny that this is what I told her, that he's in Florida. Earlier this year, that was the plan for this holiday season, to go down there to see his family. At one point, we thought there would be a baby to pass around. It's something I've tried to tamp down in my memory, pushing it away so hard it must have spilled over the edges in a lie I don't even remember telling. "You could have just asked me," I say, my voice so quiet I don't know how she hears me through the masks.

"Should I have to ask?" she says. I know she would have told me if something were off with her and Brian; I know because she always has. Brian never found out about Colin, and in that way, I know her better than her own husband does.

I look down at my shoes—ugh, my shoes! They're black motorcycle boots and I love them, but they look so ridiculous with this dress. "You and Brian can make it work through some pretty crazy situations," I say, waving my hand around the room. "We couldn't do that."

"We can do stuff like this," she says, mimicking my gesture, "because we are so strong together. Our marriage has never been better."

"We're very different people," I tell her. It's a cliché thing to say, but also, it is an admission.

"But I'm right? You and Mitch aren't together anymore? And you weren't going to tell me?"

I don't confirm or deny. She's wearing a polar bear head. She brought this on herself. I can deflect all this so much more easily than if I had to look her in the eye. Zoe says things like, *Brian is my rock*, and *Children are a blessing*. She wanted me to marry Mitchell. She's wanted me to marry everyone I've ever dated. I can read her anger in the shift of her hips and the restless way she moves her fingers on the stem of her glass.

"Fine," she says. "Don't say anything. But you get to have fun in the city all the time." I can picture a certain haughty face she makes when she talks about *the city*. "Don't be a prude."

Am I being a prude? Sort of. But it's not really the sex or whatever is going on here that is bothering me. It's the manufacturing of transgression. It's like I've wandered onto a movie set and I don't want to act. I sure don't want to be filmed.

Zoe turns to walk away. "Let us have this."

"You can have it!" I say.

*

An hour or so later, I am in a chair in the living room, champagne flute perpetually refilled, finally inured to the sights around me. Or, perhaps it's the absence of sights I'm inured to; for all the debauchery that is clearly going on, these burglars and fish and bears are discreet. I haven't seen so much skin as I've heard the click of doors, the murmurs of two suburban parent-animal hybrids linking elbows and scurrying off down the hall, leaving and returning in endless combinations. A cat and a mouse disappear, a mouse and a devil return.

I've not been drinking much lately, so the champagne could have hit me hard, but it is being gentle, making me swimmy and still. My stomach isn't even acting up like it usually does when I drink. Perhaps someone has been taking mercy on me by keeping the expensive stuff in my glass. After people start to get into the groove of the night, they stop bothering me, stop bothering *with* me, and as would only be possible here, I settle into my flamingo mask and disappear.

I'm using the mask one way, but everyone else here seems to be using it another. It's like they can't be themselves in their regular lives, not out in the open. They need something between them and the world to be able to go after what they secretly want. I guess there's nothing wrong with that. Masks can be more about revealing than concealing. That used to be all I wanted, right? Something to cover my face, to keep me shielded from the male gaze, like Val used to go on and on about. To be myself, unobserved. Back then, when I was younger, I hid behind the screen of my hair to feel free. But here, in this mask, I don't feel free at all. I didn't choose this. I don't take it off, though. How could I?

At one point, Brian pops his panther head out from behind a door and salutes me; at another, I see Zoe duck into the bathroom. When she comes out, I almost call to her. But I'm not fast enough, and she's gone as quickly as she appeared.

Then, the fish-woman drapes herself over the arm of my chair. I shift a little to the left to make sure no part of me touches any part of her, making sure no invitations are issued or inadvertently accepted. Although, I don't know. I've already decided I like her. Is she just being nice to me—a friend—or is she flirting? Should I flirt back? "It must be after midnight," she says. "Was there a countdown I missed?"

"If there was, I missed it, too," I say. Will this year just be a continuation of the last? Is it always that way?

"I guess everyone's having too much fun," she says. She clinks her glass with mine and says, "Cheers! Happy New Year!"

I look at her and see myself, again, in her scales. She could be anyone or no one under there. Maybe it's the bubbles from the champagne causing words to fizz up, the very same words I was glad Zoe didn't try to extract from me. She may have figured out that it's over with Mitchell, but she didn't figure out this. I ask, "Do you know what a D&C is?"

"Gynecologically speaking?" she asks.

I can see my orangey beak as I nod. "Wanna guess how many I had in the last year?"

"I don't," she says.

"One that was unavoidable," I say. "One that was elective."

I cough, like the words had been stuck in my throat. Immediately, I wish I hadn't said anything, and I think she can tell. She runs her hand, lightly, up and down my arm. I shiver, but it feels good.

"Elective, huh," she says. "My husband talks about the election all the time. He's on the town board."

I'm so grateful to her for changing the subject. "Something about the suburbs," I say, "is that it seems like a lot of husbands and wives vote differently from each other. I'll never get that. Zoe and Brian? Different politics. How do they get into bed together at night?"

"I take it you and your husband vote the same, then," she says.

"Except that last time." That's the thing with parties: even the most momentous decisions can be reduced to a quip. I'd already moved out when I discovered I was pregnant again. I knew, though. Not that I was pregnant—there were loads of signs that I missed—but I knew that I couldn't have a baby with Mitchell. It was a momentous decision, yes, but not a difficult one. The difficult part was telling him. Louise didn't think

I should have, but Val—she knew I'd never be free of him if I didn't. I'd always have felt that secret between us. Now, at least, there's nothing.

There were times in the last year when I would be driving home from dinner with Zoe, leaving the diner with a pile of mozzarella sticks in my stomach and thinking, as I passed our high school, that all those kids, all those shitty kids, got to be born. All their shitty parents got to be parents. I'd drive by the school and wonder if I should have told Zoe what was going on. It wasn't fair to her, to sit there across the table and pretend I was living a totally different life than I was. I think that people don't talk about their miscarriages enough, but I just didn't want to with her—I didn't want to! I didn't want her to cry. I didn't want to unleash a flood of forwards: inspirational videos, listicles of tips and tricks, rosy testimonials from women who'd had it happen to them. She would have been a font of optimism and I didn't want to hear it. Val's sardonic comments and Louise's cashmere slippers? I wanted those. I didn't want platitudes. To be fair, I can't be sure that's how she would react. I think she'd probably say she's pro-choice. Would she definitely have told me if she had an abortion? A miscarriage? I think so, but I don't know. Truly. I could still tell her. I could.

The fish-woman is still sitting with me, her energy and attention oddly sustained for any party, let alone this one. "Do you have kids?" I ask.

"I don't," she says.

The ensuing silence between us grows uncomfortable as we both struggle, I think, to figure out what to say next. She isn't touching my arm anymore. Should I touch hers? I futz with my mask to get to an itch on the side of my nose, pulling it this way and that before patting it back into place. "Wouldn't want to let my identity slip," I joke.

"I hate to say it," she says. "But I do recognize you."

I sink a little deeper into the chair. "I know you?" I ask.

"Well, at least I think so," she says. "If you are who I think you are. Also, I'm sorry, I do have kids. I have three kids. I felt weird saying it after you just told me what you told me, but if you figure out who I am, or if I tell you who I am five minutes from now, I think you'll know that I was lying."

I try to remember who Zoe mentions she sees. Where is Zoe? "Are you Heather Zucker? Jen Robbins?"

"I'm going to go get some air outside before my husband comes back in here," she says. She leans close, her forehead touching mine. I think she might kiss me and when she doesn't, I wish a little that she had. "This is a fun party," she says. "Go find someone to make you feel better."

"I feel fine," I say. The sliding glass door fogs up behind her as she steps onto the back porch. I haul myself to my feet, surprisingly still steady after all that bubbly, and survey the spread in the kitchen. Either no one has been able to figure out how to eat in their masks, or they're all too busy doing God knows what with each other, so in front of me there are platters upon platters of deviled eggs, sliders, and mini cheesecakes, heaps of grapes, cheese boards, and at least three bowls of chocolates. I palm a cheesecake and think, What the hell. I lift my mask so that it rests on top of my head like a beanie. My face is flooded with cool air, with the relief of being freed from the warmth and itch of pink yarn. I finish the cheesecake in two bites and chase it with one egg after another, then a chicken-salad-stuffed endive and a handful of briny olives. I eat between two and five of everything. Maybe I'll finish it all. The fish slips back through the door, with Dean Holt's hands resting on her hips. An OT who knows me: that's Laurie Heller under there.

The last time I saw Laurie was at Zoe's wedding. Laurie and I hadn't been close growing up, but she was one of the few other people from my graduating class who ended up in the city; I guess she's come full circle, back here now. I was painting and applying to grad school; she was studying occupational therapy. She'd been so excited when I told her about a juried exhibition that was going to include one of my paintings; what would she think if I told her I gave it up, grew out of it, got real? We'd compared notes about the various late-night spots we went to—all those early aughts loft parties, that one former massage parlor in Chinatown with the after-hours dancing, the cocktail bar behind the hot dog shop, the performance space with the pool up front. I wasn't particularly cool then, I don't think, but looking back, there I was, so young and full of energy at all those places that have closed, that a certain subset of people will "remember-when" forever. At the wedding, Laurie and I got to talking about how, to us, Zoe was practically a child bride, and how crazy it was that here, a mere hour away from our new home, everyone operated on such a different time frame. "She's probably going to have kids soon, too," I said, and we'd clinked our glasses in a way that said *that'll never be us*. We were half right.

I wipe my mouth, surveying the table. I pull my mask back down, covering my face as it heats up, blushing at how much I just ate—enough for all the other women here who haven't had a bite yet. If I look down, I can see that the one small triangle of exposed skin beneath the mask and above the neck of my dress is bright red; I hold my hand over it and back away from the table. Alone again, I wander the house, admiring the audacity of the décor. It all looks heisted from an eighties soap opera set: a three-foot-tall ceramic leopard beside a white leather loveseat, a literal bearskin rug, at least three unused crystal ice buckets on various shelves.

I peer out Dean Holt's window to see if he's got a pool, and as I press my face to the cool glass, I feel a hand on my waist. Then another hand, one on each side. Then breath on my neck: a man whispering, "Is this okay?"

"Brian?" I say. If it is him, I'll kick him in the balls, no question.

"Uh, no," the man says. "Unless you want me to be?"

It isn't him, and it isn't his voice. I would have noticed if Brian was wearing this particular spicy cologne. Whomever it is, I feel him against me, and it maybe doesn't feel so bad. He endears himself to me by asking, again, if what he is doing is okay. I wouldn't have thought it a bastion of consent out here, but I guess a party like this has to have rules. I need to decide what to say. The last time I had uncomplicated, agendaless sex was—I don't remember when it was. I edge my heels apart, a millimeter, a little more. "For now," I tell him.

As he lifts it up, I wish I wasn't wearing my mother's dress. What is it with me and other people's dresses?

The whole time, standing up, braced against the window frame in Dean Holt's what—study?—where I don't think the door leading out to the hall is even closed, I am going to tell him to stop in just another minute, just another minute, just one more minute. When I can tell he's just about there, I almost tell him to stop just so he won't and so I'll have a new worst thing to focus on, to replace the last worst thing and the one before that. I don't say stop. I don't say anything. When he walks away, I don't look back.

*

After, I grab a stack of cocktail napkins and clean up as quickly and discreetly as I can. The idea of going back into the kitchen or living room is an impossibility. I wouldn't be able to pick him out of the crowd here, but he knows that I'm the flamingo in the sequin dress. If Zoe saw me, if she knew, she'd think she'd been right to bring me here. If I leave now, I can get away without telling her this either, not that I've gotten away with what I haven't told her already. I've known for a long time that we aren't the friends we used to be, but it's real now that she knows it, too. I listen at the edge of the room until it sounds quiet in the hall, then scurry to the front door.

Outside, the cold of the night hits my bare arms, my knees, my still-damp underwear before it gets to my face, the flamingo providing a bit of protection. Without my coat, my phone, and my wallet, there's nowhere I can really go, but it is too cold to stand still so I start to walk. I figure I can make it around the block without too much damage done. The icy January—January!—air is cleansing as it penetrates the mask and pours into my skull. It feels both good and bad to start sobering up.

In the distance, I see a police car and, breathless, duck behind a tree until it is out of sight. That police officer is long gone, retired and living a few states away now, but the blue-and-red flash of lights will never not bring him back for me. Like Zoe never told Brian, I never told Mitchell; if he knew, he would say that that was part of the problem with us.

The houses I pass are not all as new and garish as Dean Holt's. Some are more like the one I grew up in, late-seventies split-levels. Some are grander, more tasteful. Plenty of them are festive with Christmas lights, windows glowing with their own parties, likely none as strange as the one I just left. There aren't many cars on the road, but before I get too far, behind me, I hear one slowing down. I turn to see a stretch limo, and I don't know what comes over me, but I lurch at it, mask on, as if I can scare it away. Undeterred, the driver rolls down the window. He's in his fifties, with slicked-back hair and a bow tie; I can't tell if he's in costume or not. He says, as if I look like any old damsel in distress, "Miss, can I help you with something?"

I sigh and roll up my mask so he can see my face. "Just taking a walk," I say. From inside the limo I hear the pulse of dance music. I crane my head, trying to get a look at who's in there. Then one of the tinted back windows opens and a blond teenager with electric-pink lipstick sticks her head out.

"You looked like something from a horror movie," she says.

A boy angles in next to her. "It's awesome," he says.

Another girl, with what seems to be an ironic tiara tangled in her wild, curly hair, pushes in next to the first and asks, "Are you being trafficked?"

One of the boys says, "I don't think rich white ladies get trafficked in our town?"

"What makes you say I'm rich?" I ask.

"You aren't?" he says.

"Depends who's asking," I say. "Where are you going?"

It's only a moment or so later that they've convinced me to get in. It really is too cold to be out with no coat. I'm wedged on a bench seat with two kids; three more face me. The limo driver seems genuinely worried about me but the kids, they're looking for a story.

"My mom won a six-hour limo rental in a raffle," the tiara says. "So we're taking a ride." She lowers her voice. "Do you have any coke on you? You look like you do."

"Thanks, I guess," I say.

"She's old enough to be our mother," one of the boys whispers, elbowing the tiara.

"I'm nobody's mother," I say.

Their mothers are probably inside Dean Holt's house, wearing cat masks and disappearing into bedrooms together. Their mothers are the ones with the cocaine. But they don't know that. They don't think about their mothers—only each other, only themselves.

Before I ever met Mitchell, before I ever left here, I used to spend New Year's Eve with Zoe. When we were fourteen, we went to a party at the house of a boy she knew from her church youth group. He was seventeen, although my parents didn't know that when they said I could go. I was wearing this blush velvet shirt, and a lotion that had little sparkles in it. Zoe had her first kiss at eleven, but I hadn't had mine yet, not until that night, not until all the boys, there must have been ten of them, wanted to kiss us at midnight. It could have ended as one kind of story, the kind so many girls have, the kind both Zoe and I do have now, but not that night. The ball dropped and we spun around the room. We kissed them all. The first one was this soft, quick peck, our lips misaligned. Someone in the middle, his tongue tasted like lemon-lime soda. We didn't even drink that night. Every kiss seemed better than the last. We both got what we wanted, no more and no less than what the other one had. My mother picked us up at 12:05, and, in the backseat, we leaned our heads together, so in love with the night and each other and the rest of our lives.

"You're going to think back on this night," I say. The kids are tangled together, heads on shoulders and arms wrapped around waists. "Years from now. That New Year's Eve in the limo."

They look at one another, their faces so bright and alive. They don't know what I'm talking about, and they don't care.

The girl with the tiara leans over and plucks the mask from its perch on top of my head. As she rolls down the window, I see my reflection slipping past: my bare face, my messy hair. She reaches her arm out into the cold rushing air and lets go. She shouts at the driver to turn up the music. The kids all sing along. What the hell. I join them.

THIRTY-FIVE
Valerie, 2013

BERRY IS RECKLESS WITH HER BODY. Her toddler clumsiness gone, her chub gone, she is wiry and wild. At five and three-quarters years old, she has chosen to be the wind for Halloween.

"How about a witch riding her broom in the wind?" I'd suggested. "Something people might recognize." I'd been worried she'd be upset when no one knew what she was. She had a history of Halloween tantrums. But she'd been steadfast; she didn't want to be a thing windblown or windswept, she wanted to be the wind itself. So here she is, leaping and shouting, "OoooOOOoooo," and flinging herself from tree stump to sidewalk to front stoop, unidentifiable in a swirl of colorless tulle. She pounces, overtaking the stairs to our neighbors' doors in single bounds. She soars across concrete and stone, her head skimming iron grates, and her knees just avoiding scrape after scrape. I am not in costume, just a mom giving in to reflex as my arms shoot out, again and again, to break her fall. If I stand too close, she swats at me, diaphanous fabric shimmering around her furious hands.

If she falls here, in our new town, it's likelier to be on a lawn than it would have been back home. In the city, I mean. I guess I can't call it home anymore. We trick-or-treat in the neighborhood that abuts ours, where well-tended yards halo the houses. We have only a small patch of grass out in front of ours. I'd planned to let nature claim it, letting whatever weeds and shrubs and flowers that wanted to take root grow, but then someone told me about all the ticks, how I'd have to keep the lawn trimmed short or keep Berry out of it for her health and safety, so no rewilded wonderland for us. A nice outdoor space: that was one of my must-haves if we were going to move to the suburbs. That, and a basement and two bathrooms. We did wind up with the bathrooms—two and a half actually, so at least there's that.

I'd always said I'd rather die than leave Brooklyn again, but then Berry didn't get into our zoned public school for kindergarten. The school right down the block, the one that touted itself as the heart of our neighborhood. The only one we ranked on our application, after reading a very convincing article forwarded by Taline regarding race, privilege, resources, and schooling. I didn't even know it was possible to be shut out of your own zoned public school in New York City, but it is. Overcrowding. I stared at the letter for a long time, the one letting us know where she'd been assigned, and felt the rejection harder than almost any in my life. More than a rejection, it was like an ejection from the city. The idea of hauling my five-year-old forty minutes in either direction to go a random school, that's what tipped me. I didn't say I'd move, but I said I'd go to a few open houses. A few kindergarten tours. It was what Marc always wanted, and it seemed like all signs were pointing to the exit.

At the same time, Berry and I ran into a friend of a friend from college in the produce section of our grocery store and she mentioned that Elliot and Tova's kid was about the same age as mine. Were they always together? she asked me. Didn't you and he have a thing? I stood, holding half a cut purple cabbage as Berry snuck forty dollars of fruit into our cart, stupefied at the thought. Were they always together? Did that explain everything? Did they have a five-year-old, too? I told her I didn't know. I didn't know the answer to any of that.

At the end of that conversation, I had it on what seemed like good, albeit third-hand authority that Elliot and Tova lived in New Jersey now, near a university where they were both professors. Rutgers? I asked when she said she couldn't remember which school. I tried to sound casual as I prompted her. Montclair? Drew? Maybe, she said. I figured that we'd want to live near a college, too. I asked Marc: That would be a good idea, right? I made a list of towns.

At the first school information session, seated at tiny chairs around tiny tables, colorful construction paper art decking the walls, alphabet runners lining the whiteboard, I'd felt short of breath and had a burning need to stretch my legs. None of these parents' faces were known quantities. None of them seemed like people I'd want to know. I raised my hand to ask the staff presenting at the open house why they thought assigning homework to five-year-olds made developmental sense and to challenge the lack of diversity in the books crammed into the little red bin on the table. After, Marc said, "You sure know a lot about kindergarten, huh."

Tova and Elliot were at the third open house. It was still a coincidence that they were in this particular set of tiny chairs on this particular day, but I hadn't been able to stop myself—I'd googled them. Of course, neither of them was on social media, but I found where they taught and then, in the bio beneath a poem Tova had had published, was the name of the town in which they lived. It was just like Tova to publish a poem—a beautiful one—when she didn't even write poetry. My surprise was genuine when I spotted them, despite having gone to life-altering lengths to orchestrate the sighting. Best efforts be damned, I couldn't mask that I, in that moment, was altered. Marc, noticing the color leave my face, tried to hand me his water bottle, afraid I might pass out.

I waited, of course, for them to notice me. Tova was in a perfectly casual denim dress, her hair tousled, and only the suggestion of makeup. Her eyes glossed over me two or three times before widening in recognition. Elliot looked like himself still—long dark hair, black T-shirt, fleeting eye contact—but had acquired a professorial bearing, a different, adult kind of confidence. Encircling him in a perfunctory hug, I was surprised to feel my arms around a *man*. It happened, in that moment, exactly how I'd always imagined: we greeted each other like old friends.

Of course, the school they were enrolling Jules in was play-based, developmentally appropriate, and didn't assign homework until third grade. My body was so alert, I swear I could feel the blood moving through my veins. I barely caught the slow smile spreading across Marc's face when I introduced everyone and said, "We're house-hunting here next week."

Later Marc said, "And we already know some of our neighbors—what could be more perfect?" I couldn't have stood it, not telling him, so I said, "I had a feeling they would be there." And something I love about him, but don't understand, is that he said he was just glad it had worked out in the end. As if that were it: the end.

*

Marc thought it was strange that we never received a dinner invitation from them, no "welcome to the neighborhood" gift basket or post-back-to-school-night drinks. I knew we couldn't be the ones to reach out first; I pretended to be surprised we hadn't heard from them yet, too.

So when Berry rings their doorbell, and Tova answers, extending a bowl of Hershey's Kisses, I'm not expecting her to say, "We're having a few people over tonight if you and Marc want to stop by."

*

Marc and I can't decide if we should wear costumes. He's never known me to wear one. The secondhand joy I felt for Berry's first few Halloweens hasn't reached those peaks again, not since she became old enough to talk and thus old enough to turn every aspect of Halloween into an argument. This year, though, so far, has been the best in a while. Once we finally agreed upon the wind, at least she stuck with it, not like last year when she arrived at my bedside at 4:21 a.m. with a costume-related change of heart. I use some of Berry's construction paper to fashion masquerade masks and tuck them into my purse. "We can put them on if everyone else is dressed up," I say, and he kisses me on the cheek.

We forgo dinner for birthday cake and candy. Berry, delighted, laps the kitchen table shrieking and leaping, electric with excitement and sugar. We'll pay the babysitter tagging in at bedtime extra. I unwrap a delicate gold necklace—too much—and a cat-shaped coin purse, clearly coveted by the giver. I pass it to her for safekeeping and she says, zipping and unzipping, "How old are you, Mama?"

I have to think. "Thirty-five," I say. "Is that middle-aged?"

Marc shakes his head. "Only if you plan to die at seventy," he says.

*

Elliot and Tova's house is a ranch, retro in the most modern way. It's the kind of house I thought we'd be able to afford, leaving the city. We wound up with good enough, with "we can close on this before the school year starts." The slate middle step leading to their front door wobbles; Marc winks. I wink back, surprised I'm capable of it. It's a miracle I'm here, upright, and not catatonic with nerves. Perhaps I've disassociated just enough. Perhaps I've grown up.

The living room, all low-slung teak tables and orange upholstery, is already crowded, filled with couples in store-bought polyester costumes or obvious pop-culture references: a beehived singer who died a few years ago, the mafia kingpin from a television show that just ended. I can't tell if I miss Halloween in Brooklyn or if I miss Halloween when I was twenty.

Marc asks, "What if, next year, all Berry wants is a Disney princess outfit from a box?"

I say, "If I already had a drink, I'd throw it at you." He goes to find us gin and tonics. I hook the elastic I'd stapled to the paper mask over my ears. I shoot Taline a text: *I'm at a party in the suburbs, wearing a mask. What is it I'm supposed to do again? Follow a handsome man into the study?* I think she's in a place now where that will be funny to her. But she'd think it was a lot less funny if I told her whose party it is. Ever since she found out we were moving—*to their town?!*—she's been watching me for signs I'm going to blow it all up. I haven't been great at reassuring her. I tuck my phone into my bag. With half my face obscured, I lean against the back of the couch. I fight the urge to cross my ankles or hug my middle and try to self-soothe with a thought experiment instead. What if under this mask was a confident woman, a suburban woman, a wife and mother who knows what she is doing, who knows what she is all about? An editor who moved here for the space, the school, and the overall happiness of her family? Who, yes, knew the couple who owned this house back in college; isn't that funny? I stand, shift my weight, decide. I don't need to be under a mask for that to be true. I take it off and stuff it into someone's abandoned plastic cup.

Next to the cup, tucked into a shelf on the floor-to-ceiling built-in bookcase, is a yellow transistor radio. Also painted yellow, on the shelf below, is a rotary phone. I extend my hand for the drink that's materialized beside me and say, "They used to have these in their house in college."

Elliot says, "We've hauled them around ever since."

"I thought you were Marc," I say. He snorts in a way that flips my stomach: elation-indignation-elation. Elliot's not in costume either.

"Happy birthday, Val," he says.

"You remember." I knock back what tastes like a very expensive whiskey. "Am I drinking your drink?"

He leans close to me, cocking his head at an odd angle. "I didn't think we should invite you," he says. "Especially on Halloween, you know? But Tova does her own thing."

"Should we not have come?" I ask. He's put his face so near mine, I'm instantly confessional. "It's weird we're here at all, I know."

"Like, how did it happen," he asks. Or does he ask? I am not sure if he wants an answer.

"Honestly," I start, then pause. Should I be honest? I eye my discarded mask. "That you live here just seemed to confirm that this town was what we wanted. That you thought this was a good place. I didn't want to leave the city, but I thought, if you like it here, maybe I could, too."

Elliot nods along. I can smell his skin and the whiskey on his breath. He must smell my shampoo. "I told Tova you came here for us," he says. "She didn't believe it."

I'm not sure which version of the story I believe either. Maybe it's both versions, that I'm here for him but also for Marc, because Marc wants to be here, or at least a place like here. Of the houses on our street, half are filled with folks who moved out from the city when they had kids. It's not like Elliot and Tova chose somewhere we might not have wound up anyway. I finish the last drop of the drink he gave me and glance around the room. Marc is in the kitchen, laughing with one of the dads he plays basketball with on Friday nights. He gestures at his mask, sniffs a bottle of gin, and tilts it toward the other dad. Marc can make friends just like that.

"See it?" Elliot asks, pulling my gaze back to him. He leans even closer, running his finger along a silver scar from his jaw to his right ear.

"I don't know," I say. "I look at you and I see it in memory. I see it in red."

Recovering from a concussion, the reconstruction of his cheekbone, and a set of broken ribs, Elliot missed midterms and had to withdraw for the semester. He went home to Maine. This was all before texting and way before social media. I called his house and spoke to his sister. I waited to hear back. When spring semester started, I was studying abroad, and then when I returned for senior year, he, Des, and Tova were away, and then I graduated. I called his parents' house again and again. I still didn't hear back. I looked for him under flashing disco lights in Brooklyn, in the journals I read in grad school, in the presence of his friends.

"I've wanted to tell you, all this time, that I was running for help," I say. "I wasn't running away. I was so turned around. I've been looking for you, you know?"

As I talk, he's standing there listening. He's not walking away. He's not forgiving me. I have my hands open toward him, as if in supplication. His eyes flit to mine, then he reaches for my left hand and brings it to his face. I feel the raised line of his scar beneath my fingertips.

"In my head, you were a ghost. Like you existed only that one night," he says, letting go of my hand. It drops back down to my side, but we are still standing so close. "I kind of can't believe that you're real."

Tova, now dressed as a blizzard—white eyelashes, silver snowflake ornaments fashioned into a crown—and Marc, a plastic cup of gin in each of his hands, converge on us. In a snowstorm hush, Tova takes us in: the combustible proximity of Elliot and me. Marc indicates the drinks, mimes tossing them at us, as if using them to quell the flames. At thirty-five, we all know when we should laugh, and I blink blink blink as none of us do.

AFTER AMERICA
Taline, 2016-2018

SOMETIME IN SEPTEMBER, I suggest to Naveed that we send in absentee ballots and go stay with his family until it's all over. The idea of putting on a hijab in the heat of Tehran wouldn't thrill me at any other time, but in the third trimester, what would one more discomfort really matter?

"Tali, you have a brown boyfriend now. You have to understand we can't be leaving and entering the country in times like these," he says.

Watching the second debate, as the man who wants to be our president hovers behind the woman who wants the same, Naveed puts his hand on my stomach and says, "She feels what you feel, you know." I want to tell him that he can't tell me anything about my body that I don't already know, but I also can't deny that I'm too worked up. It does seem unhealthy. I cut out television, radio, and podcasts. I consume news only in print so I can't hear his voice, and so his face, while omnipresent, at least isn't animated. I just have to make it to November and then the baby will be born, none the wiser about the ordeal the country has been through.

We end up voting absentee because my due date is so close to Election Day. I have a feeling that, if we don't do it in advance, we'll wind up in the delivery room on November 8, shut out of the democratic process. When the day arrives, the baby is not yet ready to make her move, though, so we walk over to our polling place anyway, just to say we'd been there. We watch as more and more people filter into the school gymnasium. The mood isn't relaxed like it was four years ago or jubilant like it had been four years before that; it's charged and expectant. It's like everyone is in our boat: at the precipice of a very welcome change after a period of intense discomfort.

*

Two weeks earlier, for one of the last classes I taught at the museum before going on leave, I'd asked the high school teacher whose students I was working with that day if he wanted to try something. I'd partnered with him for a few years running, and he taught in an alternative school, so he was used to *trying something*. The teens were skeptical when I told them that we were going to spend the entirety of their hour-long visit looking at one artwork. I'd been experimenting with spending longer and longer times at a single work, but I'd never done just one before, and never with teenagers. I sat them on the floor in the gallery, which is something teens are loath to do, but watching a woman with an eight months' pregnant belly do it first got them down on the ground.

The piece I brought them to see was by David Hammons. He created it by first covering himself in Vaseline, and then imprinting his profile, arms, and hands on a piece of paper. He sprinkled the impression with pigment; the effect resembles a photo negative or an X-ray. His grayscale form is draped in a screen-printed American flag. It was made in 1969.

The kids got busy guessing how he created it. What did his gesture mean? Are his hands raised and pressed together in . . . a high five? a sneeze? a salute? a prayer? A prayer. Wearing the flag, was he supposed to look patriotic? Like he was in a hijab? No, more like a hoodie. Is he Black? He's Black. We talked about how they're made to salute the flag and say the Pledge of Allegiance at the beginning of each school day, even though some of them aren't citizens. I asked them why they thought I wanted to spend so much time with this old artwork, on this new day in 2016. They looked at me like, *Do we really have to explain that back to you?* They knew why.

In the last ten minutes of class, I told them the title of the artwork, *Pray for America*, and had them write down their own prayers for America, an activity I stole from one of my colleagues. They were ready to read them aloud, but instead I had them fold their prayers into their pockets. Who was I to ask for their trust? Their teacher didn't meet my eyes the whole time, which I took to mean he thought this was all going a bit too far, but when he emailed me later that day, he said it was because he was afraid he might cry.

*

Naveed and I are on the couch, with pizza, watching the results come in. I text frantic messages back and forth with Val and Louise. I think of all the canvasing I didn't do and all the buses to swing states I didn't board.

We're there in front of the TV until maybe eleven o'clock. "This isn't doing us any good, Tali," Naveed says. He takes a few of the peppermint Tums I'd been eating by the handful. Pizza was a bad idea. "Let's go to bed, and when we wake up we'll have the answer."

*

I get up at four. *Up* as in out of bed—I wasn't asleep. I don't know if the churning in my stomach is my own nerves or the baby's swift kicks. I open the news app. Naveed is behind me, looking over my shoulder. I throw my phone like it burned my hand.

*

Months later, the screen is still cracked. I'd extended my unpaid parental leave and the baby needs diapers, but Naveed has a good job—I could get it fixed.

"Are you going to keep it that way until 2020?" Naveed asks.

"As long as the camera works," I say, "I just might."

*

By the time Soraya is three months old, I've taken over fifteen hundred pictures of her. I can't delete any of them, even the blurry ones or the ones with my thumb in the frame. Everything she does is for the first time; I can't help documenting all of it. When I put her in the baby carrier and wear her to an exhibition of posthumous portraiture, I take a picture: her first visit to the Upper West Side. Being on leave, I have time to go to museums I usually can't get to when I'm spending all my time working in one.

I don't put enough thought into going to see this particular exhibition, though. The portraits, both paintings and early photographs, are predominantly of children and babies. In the eighteenth and nineteenth centuries, more than a quarter of American kids died before their fifth birthday. I stand in front of this one painting, an ethereal little girl painted as though she were still alive. I read that her tragic status is indicated by the subtle pattern of angel wings woven into the lace of her dress, and by her one bare foot—it's not that she kicked off one shoe, like Soraya often does, but that she has a foot already in heaven. I sniff Soraya's hair, focusing on the feeling of her belly pressed against mine, trying to match my breathing to hers. If she'd been born back then, would she have made it these ninety-something days? She was jaundiced when we brought her home and had to return to the hospital to bask under a special lamp. Would that have done it?

I have fifteen hundred photographs of my daughter, but some mothers—the ones who could afford it—got one painting, hastily commissioned while their baby lay more and more still. Most mothers didn't get even that.

I'm almost relieved when I find a painting of a blushing young woman—at least she got to live a bit of her life—until I see she died, not in childbirth, but three days after. That used to be common, I read; it took just about that long for the infection to spread.

There was a rally in front of a Brooklyn hospital the other day. The mother knew something was wrong, but no one listened. Her death wasn't unavoidable. In fact, something went wrong when I had Soraya, too. But I wasn't at that hospital, and I'm white, and the doctor I had, she did listen. That other mother, her portrait was on a flyer shared on the internet, not in a museum, but really it was just like the one on the wall here. She looked beautiful, and alive.

*

I got to choose my baby—the when, the where, and even the how of her birth—but it also feels a little bit divine. Louise's boyfriend Clive brought Naveed along to a dinner and I knew he was it. He wasn't heaven-sent—not that kind of divinity, but the kind I know is real: the celestial powers of New York City and dinner parties and friends of friends of friends.

*

I admit to Naveed that I hadn't been sure what he meant when he said he couldn't be leaving the country at a time like this. But the airports are filled with demonstrators, and the taxi drivers and bodega workers are kneeling outside Borough Hall.

"When I called home the other day, my auntie asked if you voted for him," he says. I don't have relatives in Iran anymore; everyone left before I was born. They were Armenians, ethnically—they still are, of course. On the phone sometimes, I try to bond with Naveed's mom over Persian dishes I grew up eating. She always tells me: *We don't make it like that.*

*

Louise says to me, "You know, Taline, so many of my friends change, like change completely, after they have children. Or, maybe not completely, but in tiny ways that make all the difference. Not you, though."

We're at a coffee shop, but we're drinking wine. Soraya is putzing around, wearing these new shoes she hasn't quite figured out yet. She can't walk without holding on to something, so she cruises from my chair to Louise's, to a strange man's, to the table. When she falls, she says, "Boom."

"You admit you were wrong is what you're saying, then." I'm teasing, kind of. Louise's had been among the chorus of voices who thought I was repeating a pattern by moving in too quickly with Naveed, like I had with Mitchell and Alex before him, and making a bigger mistake by not waiting the requisite amount of time before getting pregnant again, whatever amount of time that would have been.

She pauses before agreeing that yes, she was wrong, a pause just long enough for me to suspect she doesn't, still, quite agree. "What I'm saying is, you're you in all the ways that matter."

I nod. I feel proud of Louise's assessment, but I know that I, too, am an after.

"I think it's because I already gave up something big. The change already happened." Louise sips her wine and tilts her head. She isn't quite sure what I mean. "Art," I clarify. "Painting. I wasn't good enough." She opens her mouth to argue, but I wave her off. It wasn't that I fell short in talent, although that may have been it, too. It was the fortitude. After learning that about myself, what was giving up my body, my autonomy, my heart?

Soraya toddles over to me, digging her nails into my arm and gesturing for milk. Now that she's so mobile, so opinionated, her fingernails are even more impossible to cut. She scratched her own face this morning, drawing a line of blood across her tiny knob of a chin. I hoist her onto my lap and lift my shirt just enough that she can get her sticky little face in there.

"You're you," Louise says again, laughing, "except for that. How long do you think you'll nurse? I remember Val's goal was to make it six months, then she changed it to three months and she was counting the days."

I look down and Soraya looks up. She's learned to bat her eyelashes. "Who knows," I say. "Until she's done, I guess."

The end of nursing is as hard to imagine as the beginning. If I picture weaning her, I can't help picturing the next steps: kindergarten, driver's license, death. I don't want any of it to happen, not ever. I don't feed her quite enough at lunch so she'll still crave milk. I leave her hungry at dinner, just a little, so she'll still call for me at night.

No, that's not true. I worry that's what I do, but really, she eats until she is full, then is hungry again.

Soraya curls around me, a comforting weight on my lap. It turns out the best time to drink is *while* breastfeeding, before the alcohol has time to be absorbed. I finish my wine. Soraya continues to drink. We should all be so lucky.

*

I had a job for a while that sent me into hospital schools to do art projects with the kids. It was a noble idea, I guess, but underfunded. They assigned me to this facility in the Bronx, run by a church, for pregnant teens. They lived there together in a group home situation, taken care of by nurses and teachers and nuns. It was raining the day I went, and, driving by the fecundity of Crotona Park, I felt like I was in 1950s Ireland or something.

When I got the assignment, the coordinator at my job said there would be fifteen girls and they wanted to do a textiles project. "Matching onesies and T-shirts is what their group leader suggested," she told me. Then she said I had a budget of one hundred dollars. I said that wasn't enough for a project like that, especially not one starting next week. I could maybe find the T-shirts and onesies for that much, but then there would be nothing left for other materials. She rattled off a list of places I could get T-shirts for as little as five dollars apiece. I protested as politely as I could, but I wanted to scream, *Do the math!* I arrived at the facility with the T-shirts and onesies, which did in fact use my entire budget, as well as a plastic tub I usually filled with soapy water to wash my floors at home, a bag of rubber bands, and a few packets of powdered fabric dye I begged off of a friend.

A nun in street clothes and a blue veil greeted me at the door of what felt like a rehab clinic or nursing home; it had those same industrial green walls and linoleum floors. She had me sign in, peered at my supplies, and said, "We want you to make matching mother-child outfits, to get them excited about the babies. You know, where the mother's shirt says 'Mama

Bear' and the baby's says 'Baby Bear,' with pictures of bears on them. Real cute? Like that."

By this point, I could see the girls, all gathered around a table, watching a court show on television. It was eleven in the morning.

"This is during school hours," I said. "We're going to talk about ratios when we mix the dye and the global history of pigments."

The nun was rooting around in a drawer. "I have some markers I bet you can use to write on the shirts," she said.

I accepted the markers and went in to meet the girls. One of them was telling this story about how, for her baby shower, her boyfriend had ordered a life-sized cardboard cutout of her for everyone to sign. The other girls thought this was the height of romance. They turned to look at me, their interloper, weighed down by this dumb box of T-shirts.

"These are for you," I said, putting them on the table. They all came over and started to riffle through the box, looking for their sizes. None of the shirts were their sizes, of course. Where was I supposed to get maternity shirts on such short notice? I wasn't in a position to provide these kids with knowledge, or skills, or with even an hour of fun. So I told them to enjoy and then I left.

I would have quit over that assignment, if I'd been confronted about my choice to walk out that day. But, as far as I know, the girls didn't care, the nun didn't complain, and, for years, I hardly remembered it happened at all.

*

One Saturday, Naveed takes Soraya along while he volunteers at a legal clinic, putting his Farsi to good use as a translator. It'll be nice to have her there, he says. She'll disarm people. Make it all less stressful. I'm tempted to go, too—hearing him speak Farsi on video calls with his family always brings back memories of overhearing my mother on the phone, long ago, mixing Armenian and French and Farsi and English, a strange concoction of languages only decipherable to her, her parents, and her sister. Now that her parents are gone, she and my aunt speak English.

I come to my senses and decide to take advantage of the empty apartment instead. I have a bath, clean the floors, and get a Crock-Pot of beans going. Without Soraya underfoot, I am astounded at my productivity. The day is young. I get a strange old itch in my fingers and dig out, from the back of the closet, a drawing pad. No charcoal to be found, so I make do with Soraya's ergonomic toddler crayons. I sketch our lone houseplant in purple.

Naveed comes home with Soraya sleeping on his shoulder and a series of small, greasy handprints on the front of his button-down. He doesn't want to talk about it.

*

Sometimes, there is good news. Louise sends me a birth announcement welcoming her nephew, little Étienne, born via surrogate, after half a decade of wanting. He's small and pink and loved.

*

We're coming home from getting some lunch on the first warm day in a while. Winter was never so long before having a baby; the days cooped up inside stretch on forever, with Soraya looking at me every day as if I am to blame for the sudden, prolonged disappearance of the park from her life. The mercury hits fifty degrees, and we're out the door. Our landlords, an elderly couple who've lived in the unit below ours since the seventies, have their garage open, airing it out. Naveed snakes his arm around Soraya, who I am wearing in the carrier, and pinches my side. There in the garage, alongside all the detritus of their lives, are the paper scraps of ours. Cardboard is bundled and stacked to the ceiling. I see the boxes for Soraya's Pack 'n Play, car seat, and bassinet tied together; items we received and set up at least a month before her birth. I see a small, neat stack of jewel-toned boxes from our frozen meal kick; we'd discovered this one brand that tasted remarkably good and ate them for a month or two straight until one night the microwave sparked and popped, a half-frozen pilaf sacrificed inside. Naveed thought we'd cook more real food if we didn't replace the microwave, but instead we order in five nights a week. The red-and-green-striped boxes my mother used to wrap our Christmas gifts are in the middle of a pile near the door.

Upstairs, Naveed says, "Are they keeping tabs on us? Tracking our purchases? Is that some ICE shit?" He's pacing, scratching the back of his head, and Soraya is chasing after him, pacing, too, but she trips over her own small feet so much, he's lapping her. She's going to start saying *shit* any moment. I let him run through some theories, each one less probable than the last.

"I get it," I say. "I do. But I think it's probably that they're just weird. Right? Sweetie, they're just weird."

He opens a beer from the fridge and nuzzles Soraya, holding it up to her mouth so she thinks she's taking a sip. She doesn't understand how cans work yet; we can still fool her that she's sharing.

"I guess we'll see," he says.

*

Naveed's work insists he go to a conference in Korea. I've been volunteering as a translator, he tells them. I was born in Iran. I can't be leaving the country in times like these. But his company says the same thing I did at first: you're being paranoid. They tell him, *Get on the plane.*

*

In the eighties, every time my family flew, we would have to budget in two extra hours because my mother, who still had an Iranian passport back then, would be pulled into some interrogation room for questioning, and our luggage would be unpacked and sniffed. "I loved seeing the German shepherds at work," I tell Naveed. "My mom said we were special, getting a visit from the special airport dogs."

"How old were you when you figured out what was really happening?" he asks. It is the night before he leaves.

I weave our fingers together, touch my forehead to his. "Thirty-six," I say.

"I hate to remind you," he says, "but you're thirty-eight."

"Oh yeah," I say, like I made a mistake. But no. I was

thirty-six the first time I flew with Naveed. Walking through security with him, it was like my memories changed color. I hadn't said anything then; I was embarrassed that I hadn't put it all together before. I'm still embarrassed.

We almost drift off, wrapped around each other, breathing each other's breath, but then the radiators start clanging, the heat starts blasting, and we kick off the covers, roll apart, and fall asleep. When I wake up, he's already left for the airport.

*

Val comes to see me while her daughter is at school. Soraya and I wait for her outside all morning, drawing with sidewalk chalk, inspecting rocks. I jump out into the street anytime someone tries to snag the spot that opened up just in front of our apartment, waving them along. When she arrives, Val does an expert job parallel parking. Stepping out of the car, she says, "Still got it! The other Jersey moms don't even drive in the city."

"Are you a Jersey mom now?" I ask, hugging her tight. "That's how you identify?"

"I mean," she says. "No. No! That makes me sound like a cow." Soraya takes her hand and pulls her toward our door. Val's wearing her same clog boots, which are still cool all these years later. I follow, carrying bags upon bags of hand-me-downs she brought for Soraya. I would have told Val we don't have room to store them—we won't need size 5T for years!—but she buys such nice brands. We'll find the space somewhere.

Upstairs, as Soraya gets into a stash of shoes, chewing on a well-used sneaker we really probably didn't need secondhand, Val says, "You remember—the baby phase was really rough for me. I was so consumed by Berry that I felt like I didn't even have myself for company. I couldn't wait for her to go to school, to need me less. I feel like I'm just starting to enjoy being a mother."

"With me, I feel like I'm constantly in mourning," I say. I pour her a cup of Naveed's stash of vibrant-red sour cherry tea, take a puckering sip of mine. "I am so in love with her at every stage, but I'll never meet newborn Soraya again. I'll never see her at six months again or experience that moment with her again when she finally figures out that the baby in the mirror is her. I just want another day with each of those people, you know? She keeps disappearing on me."

"Are you crying?" she asks. "Honey."

"Naveed's away on business," I say. "It's just been me and the baby for a few days, so I'm a little weepy, I guess."

"Away where?" I see her recoil as she tastes her tea.

"It'll be fine," I say. "He won't get detained. It'll be fine."

"Detained?" She takes another sip. Maybe I imagined the wince.

"I have his friend's number, the lawyer, just in case," I say. Sam's card is in my wallet, even though his number is also in my phone and on the fridge. "Sometimes I wish it was already 2020, you know? So we could put an end to some of this. But how can I wish away those years? Soraya will be four by then."

Val nods. "And who's to say 2020 won't be worse, right? Do you want me to stay with you? I can call Marc and let him know."

Now I wince. I didn't expect her to take me seriously. Or, I didn't want her to. I thought she'd comfort me. I figured she'd say there was no reason to worry. I change the subject. "How is Marc?" I ask.

She smiles. "Oh, he's okay," she says. I never would have thought it, but it makes perfect sense that finding Elliot again, that basically moving in next door to him, was the best thing that Val could have done. I always thought she should forget him, but no—getting to know him, that was what she'd needed all along. "Marc is good."

*

I wear one of Naveed's sweaters around the house, the way we used to put one of my shirts in the bassinet with Soraya, hoping the familiar smell would comfort her into taking better naps. He sends me messages a few times a day, pictures of what he's eating and a shot of himself behind a podium, wearing a slick, beautiful suit and looking brilliant. I'm distracted, checking my phone incessantly for dispatches from him. Soraya takes the opportunity and runs with it, stashing half her peanut butter sandwich behind one of the couch cushions, scribbling a full crayon mural on the back of the bathroom door. I make the mistake of cuddling her too long at bedtime the first night he's away, breaking protocol just the once. The next night, she screams when I try to leave the room like she hasn't since our second successful bout of sleep training. She's too smart for the T-shirt trick. She knows when I'm not there. I lie down on the floor, holding her hand between the bars of the crib.

After six days, I watch the notifications ping on my phone, updates from the airline tracking his progress as he flies home.

His flight has landed. But no text from him, no phone calls, hours pass: no Naveed.

I carry Sam's card with me from room to room. Soraya grabs it and I give myself a paper cut retrieving it intact. I call the airline and get put on indefinite hold. The internet just tells me the time the flight was supposed to land, same as the text, but was it updated? Is it accurate?

In the kitchen, I fish around in the cabinet and find a granola bar for Soraya. She gnaws at it, waving the crinkly wrapper like a flag. I leave a message for Sam. Now even Soraya gets it. She plays quietly with her toys, eyeing me, from time to time making her way over to place a hand on my knee or to ask to nurse even though she's not hungry. I twist my fingers through her curls, waiting for the phone to ring.

*

Sam is the one who figures it out. "The plane is still in the air," he says. "They were delayed on the tarmac, and for some reason the computers didn't update." When Naveed finally arrives, hours and hours later, I'm dead asleep. In the morning, as always, we awake to the sound of Soraya rousing on the baby monitor.

"You didn't even wait up," Naveed says, pouting. "You weren't worried?"

*

Soraya is just starting to talk when I take her to a march. Or I plan to take her, but by the time she is up from her nap, wrestled into her winter coat, and hauled onto and off of the subway, I wind up taking her to meet Val and Berry at a bar where they've gone after they marched. I make a big deal of our half-block walk there from the subway: a march in miniature. Soraya uses her limited vocabulary to count our steps: one, two, free.

I'd also planned to make protest signs. Naveed asked our landlords for some cardboard, if they had it, and they sent him into their garage to choose what he wanted, seemingly without a second thought. Then he got called into work, and I never got around to making my own, busy as I was helping Soraya with hers: squirting fingerpaint, naming colors, reveling in her full-body exploration of the materials. Now she parades through the bar waving it—covered in footprints and not quite dry—exuberant and shouting "cheese" for picture after picture.

"She's so big," Val says, handing me a beer and taking a sip of her own. Berry leads Soraya around by the hand while holding her own sign: THE SCARIEST THING ABOUT SCHOOL SHOULD BE MY GRADES. She shouldn't be old enough to know what this march is about, but she is—she's been doing lockdown drills at school for years now. Val clutches my arm. She's already had a drink or two. "I can't stop thinking about their mothers," she says. "What it must be like to remember holding this newborn, worrying over diaper rash. All the hours reading about potty training methods. Or you lost your grip on them in the ocean once and thought it was the worst moment of your life. Years slathering them in sunscreen, worrying about skin cancer. Years worrying instead of just enjoying them. And then one day they go to school and this? What happens to all of those memories?"

I take Val's hand from my arm and hold it. I have a smudge of paint on my thumb. It might be fingerpaint, or it might be oils. So far, only Naveed knows that I've been painting again. When Soraya is napping, I go to the easel in the corner of our bedroom, uncover my palette, and pour some mineral spirits into a little dish. I'm painting Soraya, while I still have her. Not that she's mine even now, not really. I paint from photographs, pulling up her sweet face on my cracked phone screen. I paint and time slows. I paint and time stops.

*

On the street, someone is beating a drum. The last of the marchers are still out there. Berry steers Soraya over to the window where a small group of children has gathered. They're bopping along with the music, bouncing at the knees. They take off their shoes to dance. Val and I are delighted and laughing. Then Soraya slips in a puddle of beer, her little stockinged feet skating out to the sides, and she's down. Her diaper-clad bum hits first, then her head. It happens slowly, more a function of her lack of coordination than anything; she's not really hurt, but that doesn't keep her from screaming. She doesn't know what happened, but she knows how she feels about it. Berry hovers over her, unsure what to do. Val and I dash across the bar, and I scoop her, beer-soaked and thrashing, onto my shoulder. Val hugs Berry to her side. I can tell she's thinking she's glad that's not her anymore, but I don't mind. I pluck off Soraya's wet socks, pat her back, and kiss her sweaty, furious head.

Berry looks between her mom and me. "When a kid gets hurt, most people tell them, 'You're okay, you're okay,'" she says.

"But my mom never does, and you don't either."

"Well, because she's not okay," I say. I use the corner of my shirt to mop the tears from Soraya's face. "Are you?"

She grabs my shirt and bites it, still angry.

*

We make it home just in time for bedtime. I draw the curtains, power up the sound machine, and surreptitiously remove half of the zillions of stuffies that have accumulated in the crib while Naveed brushes Soraya's teeth and gives her a quick sponge bath to remove any lingering beer smell from her feet. We read all the books, sing all the lullabies, and give all the kisses. Then Naveed says good night and I curl up on the fluffy rainbow area rug, halfway between the baby and the hall. I've made a little progress in getting her back into her routine. I don't have to hold her hand while she falls asleep anymore and I've inched a bit farther away each night. Tomorrow I'll be almost at the door. But tonight I'm here, in the dark, listening to her sigh and babble to her threadbare bunny and count her toes. Tonight, we are both asleep before she gets to ten.

ACKNOWLEDGMENTS

IT WAS SUCH A WONDERFUL, WELCOME SURPRISE that my editor, John Darcy, read through the entries for Noemi Press's prose contest and selected my manuscript as the one he wanted to work on. I am so grateful to him and his gentle guidance.

When, in my first meeting with Sarah Gzemski and Carmen Giménez, I said something like, "But, this book isn't really a novel and it isn't really a short story collection…" and they said, "Yes, true, so what?" I knew my book was in good hands. Immeasurable thanks to them and to Suzi F. Garcia and Anthony Cody for the work that they did and do at Noemi Press.

Caroline McAuliffe's art was an inspiration as I wrote this book. I'm thankful for her trust and generosity in letting us use *Pink Hair* for the book cover. Thank you to Steve Halle for the book design.

Ashley Lopez excavated the title *Choose This Now* from a line in the story she selected to be published in *Pigeon Pages*; stories from this book also appeared in *The Georgia Review, Bennington Review, Joyland,* and *Assignment.*

This book exists in no small part due to the *Artist Residency in Motherhood*, Lenka Clayton's idea for a self-directed, open-sourced residency. Amy Shearn and Stella Fiore started the lively, dedicated, and supportive Cut and Paste ARIM group, which is what got me writing again after having a baby, and then kept me writing through pre-school fails and the pandemic. Much of this book was written in Stella Fiore's backyard and then at the Staten Island residency house she so kindly opened up to us. I'm afraid to leave out anyone, so I won't name all the incredible ARIM folks who were so important to both the book and to me, but I am indebted to them.

These stories' earliest readers were Sara Weiss and Apryl Lee and their latest were Julia LoFaso and Helen Georgas. I couldn't do without the feedback and friendship of these brilliant writers. Helen is also my weekly accountability partner; our check-ins have been and continue to be an essential space for processing aloud and together the work that we're usually doing quietly and alone.

Thank you to the group chats: Sara Weiss, Apryl Lee, and Jocelyn Cox; Helen Georgas, Nicole Miller, and Nicki Pombier; Lindsay Lewis and Genevieve Wolff; Debbi Stein, Stephanie Joson, and Lindsay Sullivan; Sally Paul and Lisa Libicki. Thank you to Lauren Waterman, Zinaria Williams Liu, Kate Overgaard, and Miranda Beverly-Whittemore for all the writing (and other) texts. Thank you to Ananda Lima, Marcy Dermansky, Bethany Ball, and Lydia Kiesling for your words. Thank you to Kelly Sullivan for telling me that story—I asked if I could use it and I did!

Thank you to Sunnybabies 2017 and all of my playground colleagues, particularly Julie Schwartz Webb, Eric Webb, Chantal Clarke, Carla Wesby, Tomás Diaz, and Kim Diaz, for being able to talk parenting and art-making in equal measure, and to Mark Krotov for your advice.

Thank you to the teachers and staff at PS361Q.

I am very lucky to have the family I do: Carol Selzer, Michael Tull, Joe Selzer, Jane Selzer, Gregory Haroutunian, Jenn Morrill, and my nieces, and especially my ever-supportive parents Jilda and Vahram Haroutunian. Many thanks to my sister-in-law Jamie Selzer, who in addition to being a great friend is also this book's stellar copyeditor.

Dan Selzer is my favorite, always. Thank you for holding down the full-time job, for filling our lives with art, music, and laughter, and for being the best partner. Opal Judith Selzer probably helped me write this book more than anyone else. I love you, puppy friend.

Nicole Haroutunian is the author of the story collection *Speed Dreaming*. She lives with her family in Woodside, Queens in New York City.